Of Sun & Moon

Midnight Guardian Series Book 1

Bryna Butler

DEDICATION

To my mother who surprises me daily with her
wisdom and reminds me to live life boldly.

Book 1: Of Sun & Moon

Teens are disappearing in a small river town in southern Ohio as Keira Ryan begins her freshman year. Kidnappings aside, her worries mount as she crushes on an older guy, her best friend starts dating a spoiled cheerleader, and the parents that abandoned her at birth arrive at her doorstep. And, oh yeah, she's a tooth fairy destined to kick some butt and bring about the end of a royal line of vicious, blood-sucking tyrants.

Over the years, humans have pieced together sightings and assumptions to create the myth of the tooth fairy. As it turns out, they were pretty much wrong.

Midnight Guardian Series
Book 2
Coming Summer 2011

Chapter 1: Colby & Keira

Colby's head was throbbing as he lay motionless on the cold, hard concrete outside. The coolness felt good on his forehead for only a moment before full awareness slammed down on him. The wind pounded against his back and a sense of urgency surged through his entire body. He tried to move an arm, but it didn't respond. His legs ignored him too. He needed to get up. He needed to do something...anything. Keira and Brooke were standing right in front of him and they were in danger. He couldn't see the cause of his alarm, but he knew it was there. He could feel danger. As he struggled to work past the pain and regain control over his body, Colby Hayes could read the word 'anyone' screaming from Brooke's lips, but nothing more.

His head continued to throb and the ringing in his ears grew more and more intense, until he opened his eyes.

"Just a dream," he whispered to himself. On his desk, just inches from his nose, he picked up the ringing phone. "Hello."

"Were you asleep? You totally were. You may be an uncle now, but that doesn't mean you're any older. You don't have to go to bed at four in the afternoon," laughed Keira.

"No, no, I'm awake."

"Uh-huh."

Colby rose to his feet, stretched, and grabbed the foam basketball by his bed. "Anyway, you were calling because…"

"I just heard about the new baby. Hey, since he's Jamie's son, and Jamie is your half-brother, he would be your nephew, right?" Keira asked. "…Or is it half-nephew? What's the etiquette on that? Never mind. Anyway, I'm totally off track. What I meant was, since you're a new uncle, are you into family stuff with the new baby…or do you want to meet at The Landing?"

Colby juggled the phone as he listened. Finally, it came to rest between his ear and his shoulder. His hands were then free to catch the ball which he clumsily tossed just before she asked the last question. Over the last thirteen years, he had lofted more than a few failed attempts at the rim mounted to the back of his bedroom door during Keira's ramblings.

"See you in ten minutes."

Colby slipped the phone into his back pocket, slid into his sneakers, and eased down the stairs. He brushed past his mother who was trying to show him the blue baby blanket that she had proudly monogrammed for her new grandchild. It had the initials ACH for Andrew Christopher Hayes.

"That's great, Mom," Colby said without a look back as he moved out the door. "I'm meeting Keira, be back later." The door slammed shut.

Colby and Keira had been best friends for as long as either could remember. This fact was proven by his mother's vast collection of videos starring the two of them, wearing nothing but their diapers. Videos, that despite Colby's constant protest, she happily trotted out at any given opportunity.

Their longtime friendship was a bit of a mystery to most, since no two people could be more opposite.

Colby Hayes was an over-achieving, small town boy. His platinum blond hair was always neatly trimmed. His clothing matched his demeanor, always appropriate and immaculate. He was never late and always did his homework. He was always as honest as a boy scout. He was perhaps a little too safe, too honest, and too responsible. Always.

However, that never seemed to concern Keira Ryan, his very best friend and complete opposite. Her long, wavy black hair bounced wildly down her back. Her favorite outfit was her old ripped blue jeans, worn-soft hooded sweatshirt and broken-in cowboy boots. She dressed for comfort, not to impress. She always spoke her mind. Her emotions were not just felt; they exploded. She loved adventure and never missed a chance to drag Colby along.

The two were like night and day. Their friendship gave them the perfect balance.

At this moment, Colby was balancing, literally, as he crossed the log that straddled a creek at the edge of his yard. After the log, it was a quick walk through the corn field, the shortest way to The Landing. On a rural scale, Colby and Keira would be considered neighbors. Of course, a country neighbor is far different from neighbors in the city. After Keira's house, the next house down the road was Colby's, but their homes were separated by a field of a little more than a hundred yards wide. The field was part of the sprawling farm owned by the Hayes family and passed down generation by generation. Colby's dad, Curt, tended the farm and rotated a variety of crops in that particular field. One year, he would choose to plant corn; the next would be soybeans or alfalfa hay. Every couple of seasons brought a new view. The field now boasted late August corn, stretching six and seven feet from root to tassel.

Colby moved through the field to meet Keira at The Landing. The Landing was not a restaurant or popular hangout. It was simply as the name indicates…a boat landing, mostly used by locals to launch their bass boats for early morning fishing or for the occasional tourist kayak or canoe.

The breeze began to pick up. The green cornstalks danced and shimmied at Colby's sides as he made his way across the field to meet his friend. He took in the warm, sweet air. It was the kind of air that only precedes a summer storm. With no one watching, he closed his eyes and stretched out his arms to the wind as he walked. A weightless, carefree feeling pulled him open as Colby took in a deep breath and let summer fill his lungs.

Soon, he could feel the ground beneath him turning from uneven, cultivated dirt to rolling gravel. He had reached the end of the field. He stumbled and opened his eyes as he stepped from the corn rows onto the gravel path which led to the river's edge.

"Thought you said ten minutes? Try fifteen," shouted Keira from the corner of the field.

Her comment rang out like a starter pistol and the two took off. Step after step, breathing harder and harder, they pushed their way across the narrow path. Keira, receiving a definite starting position advantage, took the lead. She was quickly overtaken by Colby who immediately stumbled and fell back to second.

"I win!" Keira yelled as her right foot struck the first plank of the boardwalk. She was not even out of breath.

Colby huffed as he dusted himself off and rose to his feet. It was then that the particularly colorful sunset took him off guard with its vibrant reds and oranges. The sky was ablaze falling opposite the quiet, blue waters of the river. And there in the middle, danced the raven-haired Keira, still celebrating from her recent victory. Colby wished to linger in this summer moment, but in a brilliant flash, lightning broke the sweet orange sunset.

Keira stopped when she noticed that he was not right beside her. "You okay?"

He nodded.

"Hurry up then, it's gonna rain." She grinned as she grabbed his hand and pulled him toward the shelter.

The Landing consisted of a creaky boardwalk leading to a rickety, wooden pier that sprang from the corn fields and jutted out into the river. Beside the pier was a park shelterhouse with open sides, a metal roof, a concrete floor, and stuffed with a half dozen weather-beaten picnic tables. When the river was high, the shelterhouse was flooded. When the river receded, it left behind a wake of mud and driftwood on the floor. For this reason, the structure was rarely used. Eventually, weeds and vines grew to almost entirely enclose one side. However, on most summer days, like this one, it was still the perfect spot to watch the sun set over the river. That's why Colby and Keira spent so much of their time there.

As the first, fat raindrops struck the tin roof of the shelter, Colby stretched to retrieve his flashlight from its high hiding place on the inside ledge above the entrance. He didn't need it yet. The rainclouds failed in their attempt to restrain the sunlight that was now streaming from the horizon. Instead, he tucked it under his arm and headed to his usual seat at the end of the centermost picnic table. Keira climbed on top of the same table and collapsed.

"I can't believe this is our last day of summer," she moaned to the shelterhouse rafters. "It's gone. Gone! Do we really have to go back tomorrow?"

"Well, there is one good thing about going back to school," Colby said without even looking at her. He was too busy dusting off his seat.

"Yeah," replied Keira dreamily. "William." High school junior and star football running back William Swift had been Keira's most recent infatuation.

"Hold it. I'll make you a deal. I won't talk about her tonight, if you don't talk about him."

"Deal," Keira quickly nodded in agreement. She had heard enough about the great and wonderful Brooke Banes to last her a lifetime.

Colby continued, "What I meant to say was that back to school this year means *high* school. All new challenges, new place, new people…"

"Oh boy, honors chemistry! Yipee!"

"Okay, I didn't say that."

"No, but you were thinkin' it," she giggled. He laughed too.

As the evening wore on, Colby turned on the flashlight. The conversation effortlessly moved from school, to Colby's new nephew, to what movie to see next weekend. The light began to dim as the last rainclouds rescinded and the full moon appeared. Keira glanced up at it and a chill ran down her spine. As Colby pulled his phone from his pocket, Keira's eyes were drawn to the electronic glow of its screen.

"Colby! How could you let me stay this late? Nana's gonna kill me."

"Well, she knows you're with me," Colby rebuffed in an uncharacteristically cocky tone.

"True. You *are* the most responsible young man in town," she said with a sweeping grand gesture. "Here stands Colby Hayes, a role model for our entire generation."

"Yeah, that sounds like me, but if she only knew the true *you*…"

These words cut the jovial mood like a knife. With the grace and swiftness of a lethal, jungle cat, Keira's feet hit the ground and she was suddenly standing.

"Whoa, how did you…"

She seized his left arm and lifted him to his feet. She stared deep into his eyes. "What do you know of the true me?"

He let out an unintentional yelp. He couldn't decide if this was real or some sort of practical joke. Keira continued her stare on him causing him to laugh nervously, trying to understand, until he finally decided to play along.

"I know the true you. Who else knows that you are extremely bad at Monopoly."

"What?"

"...and Hide 'n Seek," he continued. "Remember when we were five and you hid behind the living room curtains...the *sheer* curtains?"

Keira relaxed slowly and started drifting back to her old self. She let go and patted him on the chest. "All right, smart guy. I have to get home before midnight," she said as her face returned to its familiar gentle smile. She grasped his palm. "Sorry, I didn't mean to be such a weirdo. I'd better get home. See you tomorrow."

Without waiting for a response, she turned and made her exit guided by the light of the full moon in a now cloudless sky. Colby watched, rubbing his sore arm, as she disappeared down the gravel path.

Chapter 2: Mystery Loaf with Cheese

The first day of school at Valley View High was like many others. The rain of the night before had already evaporated in the late summer heat. It now held in the air, making it muggy and thick. Inside everything smelled new. The classrooms were freshly painted; the floors freshly scrubbed. The school was alive with the squeaks of new sneakers and excited chatter of friends catching up after the long summer.

Colby's mom gave him a ride to school. Keira, on the other hand, was forced to ride the bus. After a rather uneventful morning, she spotted her best friend in the hallway at his locker, his nose deeply immersed in a map of the school.

"Hey, if it isn't Uncle Hayes. How have you been, dear old man?"

"Quite well, Miss Ryan," Colby grinned as he threw the map into his locker and shut the door.

"Walk me to lunch?"

"Are you sure that you don't want to weasel your way to your sweet William's table?"

"Ooh. *My* sweet William. I like the sound of that," beamed Keira as she took Colby by the arm. They started down the hallway. "I'm sure that we can find the perfect spot so that I can stalk...I mean, keep an eye on, William and you can drool over...I mean...well, I was right the first time...drool over...Brooke."

"Very funny, but I've got my own plan."

"You don't mean..."

"I'm going to do it. I'm asking Brooke to the Fall Ball," Colby said as he dropped her arm to push through the doors at the end of the hallway.

Now, please understand, the last time that Keira witnessed Colby showing this type of social confidence was in kindergarten when he rescued her lunchbox from Jumper Johnson. The only time he ever spoke up was in class, and even then, only when called on. Colby could barely utter a 'hello' to a girl that he liked, let alone ask her out.

Shocked by her friend's new-found assurance, Keira couldn't help but let out a quiet gasp at his declaration. "And I thought you were going to say that you would try to sit near her at lunch." She gathered up her shock and patted him on the back. "This is a huge step. I'm proud of you." Really she was just thinking one thought; I hope he doesn't puke on her shoes.

The duo made their way across the crowded commons area and into the lunch line. "Yipee! Honors chem *and* mystery loaf *with* cheese. High school rocks!" Keira yelled. Colby closed his eyes, slightly embarrassed by her outburst, but not surprised.

Round tables occupied by the geeks, the jocks, the carefree, and the cool, covered every inch of the commons area. The noise of clattering trays seemed to fill the space not taken by tables. Teachers gently pushed through the gobs of students shouting orders like 'Don't cut in line', 'Only take what you'll eat' and 'No horseplay'. Their guidance was the only clarity in the total chaos. However, there was an oasis amidst the pandemonium, a wall of windows on the north side. The windowed wall made the whole space feel warm and open. Typically, Keira would choose a seat there so that she could stare at the sunny sky and daydream about being free from school. Her eyes certainly drifted that way, but a loud laugh from the object of her obsession lured her back into her mission.

Keira glanced quickly to make sure that she was not the cause of his spontaneous laughter. No, at least not this time. It was probably just a joke or some juicy gossip. She scanned the room and spotted gal pal Ann Martin eating solo at a table within a few feet of William and his friends. "Jackpot!"

Colby may have been Keira's best friend, but Ann was her best girl friend. The independent and clever Ann Martin was more level-headed than anyone Keira knew, often dispelling that old myth about the temper of girls with red hair. Best of all, Ann had a penchant for gossip. Actually, it was much more than that. Ann had a gift for getting to the truth fast. She loved hunting out a story, which made sense because she long held dreams of becoming the next Katie Couric.

Keira clearly spent more time with Colby than with Ann, but she devoted a certain amount of that time trying to set Colby up on a date with Ann. That's what Colby thought this was.

Half pulling, half dragging Colby with one hand and balancing her lunch tray with the other, Keira made her way through the commons in a beeline for Ann's table. By the time she reached the table, none other than the infamous Jumper Johnson had pulled up a chair. Keira dropped Colby's arm and plopped down beside Jumper. Ann was on his other side watching Keira anxiously. She had seen that look in Keira's eye far too often. Colby knew that look too. It was the same one that caused butterflies in his stomach. Keira scooted her chair close to Jumper with a wide grin on her face.

"Jumper, how strange, I was just thinking about you," Keira sweetly whispered. She lifted her hand and gave him a flirtatious stroke on the cheek.

"Really?"

"Oh yes, Jump," she said, her hand now running through his hair. "I just can't seem to get you off my mind."

"Now, Keira, I'm just not into you like...."

"Hush darling. I know our tragic love was never meant to be."

Ann and Colby busted into uncontrollable, howling laughter. Every student within four tables distance turned to find the source of the commotion. Keira could see a red wave wash up Jumper's neck and face to his dusty brown hair. The sight reminded her of a boiling thermometer.

"You told her already," Jumper surmised. "Real funny, Ryan. You're such a pain." He shifted his chair further from Keira, as close as possible to Ann.

"Relax, Jump, I'm only kiddin'. I love it that you two are dating. I never thought about it before, but you and Ann are good for each other."

"I think so," said Ann with a grin. She gave him a peck on the cheek.

"Yeah. Ann is smart, kind, beautiful, and funny. I guess opposites *do* attract, huh Jump?"

Jumper glared at her. "Oh, you are so gonna get it. You won't know when or..."

He stopped in mid-sentence as the double doors burst open. A confident smile spread across the face of Brooke Banes as she strode into the room. Her playfully short turquoise dress showed just the right amount of her lean body and flawless, sun-kissed skin. Long blond curls bounced at her shoulders as she walked. Brooke didn't look like your average freshman girl. She was like a real, live Barbie doll...ridiculously perfect. All eyes were on her; just as they always were.

Colby was never the type to fall for appearances. Still, Keira couldn't help but notice him, noticing Brooke. She knew he was a teenage boy, but couldn't quite understand his infatuation with Brooke, and it was definitely infatuation. More than a passing crush, he was actually working up the nerve to ask Brooke to the dance. Colby spoke of no other girl. What do you think she's really like? Do you think she's as cool as everyone says? These were just two of the hundreds of questions that Keira had quickly found tiresome. After all, he only knew her by reputation since Brooke didn't attend their middle school.

Keira liked to think that his interest was based deeper than appearance. After all, this was Colby. He wasn't into that artificial stuff. He was better than that. She preferred to assume that Brooke's recent drama had endeared her to him. Her family moved to town last spring. No one really knew her until she started dating Bobby Crimson.

Bobby was *the* guy at Valley View High. A competitive skateboarder, the bleach blonde bad boy was well on his way to being the next X-Games star. He and Brooke broke up in a very public fight at the Independence Day fireworks. She had accused him of cheating on her with one of his skoopies (Ann coined the word as a combination of skateboard and groupies). Bobby had nearly twenty skoopies. They followed him from competition to competition and even stalked him at school.

Anyway, Brooke accused him of cheating and he denied it. Her distrust was more than his monster ego could take. "You better back up and rethink. You need me, not the other way around. I can get a dozen more just like you. Just say the word, baby; set me free," Keira remembered him screaming at her in front of everyone. Brooke ran away in tears. A month later, Bobby went missing. The FBI was still in pursuit of the lead suspect, a meth-ravaged drifter that was spotted in the skate park earlier that week. Keira couldn't begin to imagine the regret that Brooke must be carrying. There hadn't been any boys in her life since the breakup, which sadly meant that a soft-spoken bookworm like Colby had zero chance.

As Brooke passed the gang's table, she smiled at Colby. To Keira's surprise, it was not just any smile, but an intentional, lingering gaze. However, it didn't even last long enough to break her stride as she kept moving until she reached her final destination…the cheerleaders table. As she sat down, the commons slowly returned to its pre-Brooke state.

Ann leaned over the table toward Keira to interrupt her gaze. She had completely zoned out, thinking about Colby and Brooke. Ann lifted her hand to cover the side of her face as she spoke.

"Did you see you-know-who sitting right over there?" Ann whispered, nodding toward William's table.

"Oh, you know, that I know, where the who-that-you-know is."

"For crying out loud, we can hear you. Is that even English?" Jumper asked with disgust. The girls just ignored him.

Keira's eyes were now set on him. William Swift was seated just a few feet away at a table with five other players from the varsity football team. He was wearing jeans and his white practice jersey which complemented his dark complexion. His muscular arms moved gracefully into huge gestures as he talked. His eyes were wide with excitement in the story he was telling. When he smiled, the dimple in his cheek showed. When he laughed, Keira felt weak in the knees. She was staring at his spiked, black hair, wondering what it would feel like if she could reach out and touch it. That's when he caught her gaze. He returned it with a quick smile, then shook his head and turned his eyes to the floor shyly.

Keira breath stopped. She quickly looked down at her tray and smiled to herself. After a few moments, when they were sure that he was no longer paying attention, Ann and Keira squealed with delight.

Their voices hit a register that the guys were sure only dogs could appreciate. For the remainder of the lunch period, the girls plotted out the best possible scenarios for matching up Keira and William. All too soon, the bell rang and students quickly dissipated into the halls.

"Catch you later, Hayes. Ready, babe?" Jumper asked. He picked Ann up to stand on her chair and turned around, offering a piggy-back ride. She jumped on and they galloped out of the commons. Colby could have sworn that he heard Jumper whinny as they pushed through the doors.

Colby walked straight to his locker and started fishing out his books and the crumpled school map for the afternoon. A few moments later, Keira wandered by and rested against the neighboring lockers.

"We've got English together this afternoon, right?" Keira asked Colby as he started to hurry away.

"See you there, troublemaker heartbreaker," he replied as he tripped spilling his books on the floor. She drifted down the hallway to help.

Chapter 3: Fairy Tales &
Other Enablers of the Ignorant

Colby was the first student to arrive in the English classroom that afternoon. Knowing his preference for the front of the classroom and Keira's preference for the back, he strategically chose a seat in the middle. As usual, Keira slid into the seat directly behind Colby just as the tardy bell rang. Jumper was seated to her right, which was a suspicious position, given that he was an equally skilled prankster and Keira was due for a little payback after lunch.

The class began normally. Roll was taken. The teacher, a handsome young man with geeky black glasses, seemed as distracted as the students. The thought of being tied up in school on this particularly beautiful late summer day was disconcerting to everyone.

"Let's get on with it people. Open your books to page 3," Dr. Tyler said with a sigh. "For these first few weeks, we will discuss fairy tales and fables."

"Great," Keira said with a roll of her eyes. Unfortunately, the comment was spouted with a bit more volume than she had intended. It reached Dr. Tyler's ears.

He looked over his glasses at Keira and picked up the attendance record. He stood quietly not taking his eyes off her. "Would you like to share your insight on this genre with the class, Miss Ryan?"

"Not really, but you asked."

Colby's mouth gaped open and his pencil dropped to the floor. Having the complete opposite reaction, the corners of Jumper's mouth pulled into a large grin. The room fell deathly quiet except for a few random giggles. The few seconds that followed seemed like hours until Keira spoke again.

"I just think that these stories…er, I guess, tales, whatever you want to call them…are ridiculous. Why would anyone waste their time to read or believe any of this garbage?"

Jumper snickered. Colby couldn't believe his ears. This was no way to make a first impression. Why was Keira goading the teacher? He slumped down in his chair so as to not intercept the cold, piercing gaze that Dr. Tyler now had on Keira.

Dr. Tyler, in a manner that was eerily calm, attempted to explain, "One man's garbage…another man's treasure, Miss Ryan." He turned to the class and continued, "These works are fiction. They are a flight of fancy, a feast for the imagination, a…"

Keira rose to her feet and slammed her hands on her desk. "Don't you mean a mockery of the truth, an enabler of the ignorant? Do stories of fairy godmothers prancing around, elves, goblins, mogdocs, and trolls really help? Puh-lease, tales of idiotic creatures like tooth fairies help no one. Oh, and are we really to believe that the poor, tragic, but brave orphan assumes their destiny only after their parents die like in Cinderella, Snow White," she shrieked. "HELL, even Harry Potter?" She smashed her fist against her textbook and the desk top fell apart, hitting the floor with a loud bang.

Even Jumper was speechless.

"Miss Ryan!" Dr. Tyler barked, showing considerably less restraint than before. "I appreciate a spirited debate. However, I do not tolerate vandalism or profanity in my classroom. You are dismissed to the principal's office. Take all your belongings with you. You may be there for quite some time."

Keira rushed out and slammed the door behind her. As Colby recovered from his shock at Keira's outburst, he finally realized what was really happening. The clue came from her last words; an orphan, like Cinderella, Snow White, Potter…an orphan, like Keira.

Yet, Keira was not exactly like those fictional characters. She was an orphan, not because of the untimely death of her parents, but because of their decision. Colby didn't know much about it, but he did know that her parents were still among the living. They were very young when she was born. A few days after she came into the world, they gave her up. She has lived with Nana ever since. Nana was a kind woman and Colby had always believed that she was actually Keira's grandmother or some other relative, even though that theory had never been confirmed. Thinking back, he realized that he never really had a solid reason for this opinion, it was just a feeling. Keira would never talk about it. She never visited or even talked about her parents. Colby had supposed that the fear of being unwanted was too terrible for even the fearless Keira to face.

Still, Keira's classroom meltdown was bizarre and it left Colby with a truckload of questions. Of all things to set her off, why was it English class? Why was the most imaginative person that Colby knew ranting about creative stories? Why was she being so closed-minded? Was she conceited enough to think of her life as a fairy tale?

Colby's insides were racing to catch up with his best friend as his body was forced to stay put. Did she need him? For once, the teacher's pet found that he was thinking of something other than the lesson. His questions collected like raindrops in a bucket and filled his head until it overflowed. There was only one person that could answer them.

When the bell rang, he darted into the hall, through the gym doors, across the library, to the principal's office. Keira was nowhere to be found. Deciding that she must have already received her sentence, Colby headed to his next class.

Still, his questions were all he could think about. There was no logic to what had happened. His mind needed it to make sense. He blocked out everything else as the scene played over and over in his head. That's probably why he didn't notice the incessant tapping on his shoulder soon after he took his seat in study hall. Escalating her attempt to get his attention, Brooke finally leaned forward and whispered directly in his ear… "Colby."

That sweet perfume ripped Colby from his distraction in a heartbeat. His spine tingled as she leaned in close again, softly brushing his ear with her cool cheek… "Colby," she called again.

He could feel his whole body tense as her breath hit the back of his neck. "Ba…Brooke. Hey, hi, I mean uh, what's, uh, what's goin' on?" Colby somehow managed to shut off the babbling by reprimanding himself in his own head.

"You're Colby, right? I heard about Keira and I know you two are close. Is she okay?"

She leaned back in her chair and Colby turned around to meet her glimmering emerald eyes. Her blonde hair seemed to glow lightly as it framed her angelic face. Her tan skin was accented by pink cheeks and lips. Dazed by her beauty, he started to answer almost unconsciously, "I hope so. I mean, I think so. She had already left the principal's office when I stopped after class."

"You don't know?"

His stomach began to tighten. All he could do was look at her. She leaned close for the second time and Colby could feel his heart racing as if it were about to pop out of his chest and sprint down the hall. He gripped the edge of his seat to steady himself.

"Keira didn't go to the office. They're furious. Dr. Tyler, Principal Murphy…they're all looking for her. They know she couldn't have gotten too far off school grounds; she hasn't had enough time. Colby, if she left the grounds, that's cause for suspension maybe even expulsion."

"She wouldn't leave. I think I know where she is."

Colby raised his hand and asked Mrs. Bethany for a hall pass under the pretense of working on his honors research project in the lab. She granted his request. Colby wasn't one for lying or breaking the rules, but this time Keira needed him.

He quickly made his way to the chem lab. Luckily, this was the chemistry teacher's planning period, so the lab was completely empty. Carefully checking that no one was watching, he moved to the back of the room and opened the wooden door to the lab's supply closet. Once inside the closet, he shut the door and turned to a large, dingy white cardboard box marked *Handle with Care: Bunsen Burners*. He shoved the box aside to uncover a small door painted with giant sunflowers and a rainbow.

This was their secret hideaway. Colby had discovered it the year before, after spending countless hours in the lab to secure his spot in the accelerated science program.

When the school was built, the district superintendent at the time included the nursery as part of the building plan. To the public it was praised as progressive and an invaluable aid for teen mothers, but privately it served as free daycare for the superintendent's five young children. So, after she retired, the nursery was closed. Eventually most of it was converted into a massive storage closet for the new lab, but this tiny space on the other side of the miniature door was useless and eventually forgotten. Colby had shown it to Keira last week, after she had convinced him to sneak off from freshman orientation for some extra exploring.

As soon as he pushed the door, he could hear the sobs of his friend. Light from a high window streamed down to bounce off her black hair. He bent down and pulled himself through the tiny doorway. By the time he entered and re-latched the door, she had gained control of her tears. He sat down beside her on the floor. Keira turned to him. She couldn't look him in the eyes. Instead, she leaned on his shoulder and stared at the wall. "I'm fine. I just...you know."

"I do," he said, even though he really didn't.

"Thanks."

It took every ounce of restraint that Colby had in him not to say more. He wanted so badly to ask the questions that had driven him to this hiding place, but he watched them evaporate as he looked into her sorrowful eyes.

"Well, I have some gossip that will cheer you up," Colby said in an effort to re-direct the conversation.

"What's that?"

Colby grinned, "I hear that Brooke Banes can't stay away from Colby Hayes. She was practically on top of him in study hall, whispering in his ear."

"No way, sounds like a fairy tale to me."

Chapter 4: A Swift Rendezvous

Colby walked Keira to the principal's office. She didn't want to and had resisted at first, but she knew it was better to face the music than to put it off any longer. Colby opened the door and Keira moved quickly to the counter to let the secretary know of her presence. Before she even spoke a word, Principal Murphy stormed out of his office with Dr. Tyler trailing behind.

"Young lady, get in my office right now," he demanded. He looked to Colby, "Thank you, Colby, for finding Keira, you should return to class now."

Keira bowed her head and moved slowly toward the principal's desk. Colby could see that Dr. Tyler was already scolding her quietly as they walked.

"Please, Mr. Murphy," Colby pleaded.

"What is it?"

Colby motioned for him to come around the counter so they could speak out of Keira's earshot. This was probably unnecessary as Dr. Tyler currently had her full attention.

"Sir, I know this is bad," he started and Murphy nodded. "But, I want you to know that she didn't go off campus. She just found a place to hide so that she could cry. She just got upset over nothing. You know how girls can be sometimes. She just got wrapped up in her own drama."

Principal Murphy put a firm hand on Colby's shoulder to signal that he should stop speaking. "Please, sit down for a minute."

Colby took a seat along the wall, parallel to the counter, as the principal began to speak to him. "Colby, you know that you are poised to be one of my star students. I appreciate that you convinced Keira to come to my office. However, I need you to understand that you are not her keeper. This friendship is quickly becoming a detriment to your high school career." Colby grimaced as the principal continued. "Take today's outburst and resulting vandalism for example. Also, I'm guessing that you were not excused from class to look for your friend. I know that you mean well, but I've seen this happen before. One day, your support of her actions will negatively impact your own future. Concentrate on yourself and your own studies. I don't want you to start off on the wrong foot. Do you understand?"

Colby started to object, but knew that it would do no good, so he simply nodded in agreement.

"Mrs. Chandeline, please prepare a hall pass for Mr. Hayes, he will be returning to class now."

With no further word, Principal Murphy turned and entered his office, shutting the door behind him.

Colby ambled down the hallway. He was not eager to return to class. He would have to explain to Mrs. Bethany why he was in the principal's office when he should have been in the lab working on his research project. He would have to withstand the looks from the other students. He would have to tell Brooke what happened. Well, talking to Brooke was never bad, he thought to himself. Maybe returning to class would be a good thing after all.

Just as he had anticipated, he entered study hall to quizzical glances. He handed the hall pass to Mrs. Bethany who also gave him a questioning look. He quickly explained by telling her that he ran into Keira and talked her into going to the principal's office since they were looking for her. The simple explanation was good enough, so he took his seat. It was not long before he felt a gentle tap on his shoulder.

"Did she really just go to the principal's office because you told her it was the right thing to do?"

"Yeah. I guess, she did."

"Impressive, Hayes," Brooke said. "I wonder if that would work with me."

"What do you mean?"

She shook out her long blonde hair as she spoke. "Well, I was just wondering if I would act on your advice so completely?" she said in an obvious attempt at flirting. Colby decided that this was the moment.

"Let's try it out," he said, low enough that it was mostly for his own ears. When Mrs. Bethany looked down to continue grading papers, he shifted around in his seat to face Brooke. He took in a quick, deep breath. "I think you should go to the Fall Ball with me."

"I guess I have my answer now. I *would* act on your advice."

She looked down at her notebook and started scribbling. Colby furled his brow, a little confused by her comment. She looked up at him with a wide grin, "That means yes, Colby. Yes, I'll go to the dance with you, but…"

"I know. I shouldn't have asked. I mean, we barely know each other. I understand, it's okay."

"Understand what? I was just going to suggest that we go out before the dance too. That way, we can get to know each other a little better. Here's my number, call me."

Colby choked out a "sure" and turned back around in his seat. "Act cool…act cool…act cool…" he ordered himself in his head as he exhaled at last.

***

The days grew shorter, the air cooler, and soon it was just two weeks before the annual Valley View High Fall Ball. For Colby and Brooke, it would be their fifth date, a double date with Jumper and Ann. Determined not to be outdone by Colby, Keira had decided that it was time to move her relationship with William Swift from imaginary status to real.

After tons of planning for the perfect moment with help from Ann; she threw caution to the wind when she was, only by coincidence, seated next to William at a pep rally in the gymnasium.

Her confidence was flowing and her patience was waning, so she decided to make the first move.

"Hey, good luck at the game tonight," she said with a flirty toss of her hair.

"Yeah, thanks, Keira," he said. He knew her name. This was a good sign. He turned to her and smiled as he continued. "Are you gonna be there?"

"Sure, I go to all the games."

This was mostly true. Jumper played on the freshman team. He was a fanatic for varsity ball and so of course, that meant that Ann had been attending all the games too. She would often take Keira with her. Keira never minded going. She actually enjoyed it. She felt that any place where she could jump, dance, shout, and eat junk food was a good place to be. The football games had all that and more.

"Well, I have to admit that I've noticed you in the bleachers," William said.

She tried to recall the last game. It was a home game. Jumper had gone shirtless, wore a red clown wig, and painted the word "GO" on his chest in school colors. Did she do anything that she might regret now? That is…besides associate with Jump?

"Really?"

"Yeah, and sometimes I go out of my way to pass by your locker."

"Oh."

This was unexpected. She had to re-think her whole approach. As she considered her next words carefully, the pep band began to play the school fight song and everyone stood. The crowd began clapping and singing along. Keira looked toward Ann for help and spotted her two rows behind, about six people away. Keira was gesturing wildly to get her attention when she felt a strong hand brush the small of her back. She turned and found herself two inches from William's nose. She jumped. He laughed and leaned to her ear.

"It's so loud. I don't think you heard me," he yelled.

She shook her head.

"I was just saying that since you'll be at the game. Do you wanna to do somethin' after…with me?"

"I guess."

"Good," he smiled as he pulled his arm back to join in the applause for the JV squad as they strode to center court.

***

At the game, Keira was with Ann and Jumper in the middle of the student section. Sitting wasn't an option. Everyone was wild, a stomping and chanting sea of red and white. The scent of concession stand hotdogs and stale popcorn floated through the air. Keira could feel her heart beat with the rhythm of the marching band's bass drums. With each thump, her heart jumped, pushing her to cheer louder and louder.

From where she was standing, she could see Colby. He sat in a much quieter section with his parents. For this game, the freshmen cheerleaders were allowed to perform during third quarter, so he was there to support his girlfriend, Brooke. It was a good thing that he was busy, Keira thought. She hadn't had a chance to tell him about her planned rendezvous with William after the game.

The football game was a real nail-biter. The score was close throughout. William played an awesome game, as well as the rest of the team. In the last seconds, a two-point conversion led them to victory. Afterwards, Ann and Jumper waited with Keira on a bench outside the locker room.

William was one of the first players outside. He looked nervous; at least that's what Ann said when she retold the story later. It amused Keira to think of how she had to beg and plead with Nana to allow her to go out with a junior. It was only two years, less than that if you considered that she was one of the oldest in her class and he was one of the youngest in his. Still, the fact that William could drive made a big difference. Nana had finally given in with one condition; Keira had to be home well before midnight.

William walked over to the bench and stood in front of where Keira was seated. He pushed his hands into the pockets of his jacket. Ann and Jumper, taking the hint from Keira's eyes, immediately made an excuse to leave.

William reached out and helped her to her feet. He continued to hold her hand as they began to stroll down the sidewalk to his pickup. Stars filled the clear sky. Fall leaves covered most of the path and crunched under their feet as they walked. The cool night air pushed gently against them.

"I'm glad you're here," William said to Keira.

The breeze lifted her hair a bit. "I'm glad I'm here too," she said biting her lip. "So, is there a plan or…" she started, pushing a few wandering strands of hair from her eyes.

"Well, I've got a couple of options for you. Lee is having a party to celebrate the win, so we can do that."

"Or?" Keira pushed.

"Or Plan B," he smiled. "If you're not into the party, we can just do somethin' quiet together like get some food and talk."

"Why not both?"

A wide smile spread across his face. His pearly, white teeth sparkled a bit under the street light and he did that thing he does, that thing that drove Keira crazy. He shook his head slowly and took a shy look at the ground. "I like the way you think," he said.

The wind picked up his ball cap. Keira caught it and replaced it on his head before he even had a chance to reach.

"And you're quick."

She shrugged and looked away. He run his fingers across her cheek and lifted her chin so that her eyes met his. "This feels right."

Wow, Keira thought to herself.

I can't believe I just said that out loud, William thought to himself.

They both looked away, but grasped hands again, this time a little more tightly.

They decided to head to Lee's first. It was a huge party. Even though she was one of only three freshmen there, she didn't feel out of place. In fact, Keira never really, ever, felt out of place. Her confidence carried her. Besides, William held her hand the entire time, so she barely noticed that anyone else was there. But, everyone did notice her. She was the recipient of many looks. Some looks were jealous, some were questioning, but most were full-out shocked. She didn't care. This was turning out to be the best night of her life. After a little more than an hour, he asked if she wanted to leave. She resisted at first, thinking that this meant the evening was over. Then, she remembered his promise for the second half of the date.

They left the party, arm in arm, and bounded into William's red Ford F250 extended cab. It roared loudly as they sped away. They stopped at the only place still open, Dairy Dog, a seasonal hot dog and ice cream stand near the high school. William ordered as Keira staked out a claim on the picnic table inside the stand's neighboring gazebo. It was sort of romantic, even for a hotdog stand, Keira thought. The top of the gazebo was decorated with twinkling, white lights. Moonlight reflected off the honeysuckle vines which twisted around its support beams. William soon returned with a tray of footlongs and shakes.

Keira grinned as he sat down on the same side of the picnic table, right beside her. "This is not at all what I expected," she said as she picked up her shake.

"Oh, I thought you said you wanted strawberry."

"No, not the milkshake, I meant the date."

"Are we calling this a date?"

She smiled and punched his arm lightly.

"So, what *did* you expect?" he pushed.

"Well, I'm an awful judge of character. So, I was afraid that you would turn out to be a total jerk. No offense."

"None taken," he laughed. "Anything else?"

"No. It's been pretty perfect."

William laughed again with that thing he always does with his dimpled grin and shy look to the ground. "Glad you think so."

"There is something else, um," she hesitated, picking at her hotdog.

"What?"

She looked up into his eyes, those gorgeous, perfect eyes. "It's cool if you already have plans, but if you don't, I was thinking about going to the Fall Ball and I want you to come with me."

"Like a date?" he smirked. "I guess I could do that."

She smiled and he leaned in. Then a shock went through her. You know the feeling. The feeling you get when everything's perfect then out of the blue you suddenly remember that you've forgotten to do something... something very important. She was feeling it right then, a second of shocking recall.

"Oh no, what time is it?"

"Quarter till midnight."

"I'm sorry, I better get home. Um...midnight curfew."

"Midnight?" He looked disappointed for a moment, then perked up. "No sweat, Cinderella, I'll get you home in record time. Can't have you grounded for the ball."

They jumped in the truck and were at Keira's front door in minutes. She began frantically searching her pockets for her house key.

"Wanna go out again before the dance? How about tomorrow?"

"Can't, I have training," Keira said in her rush to get in the house.

"Training?"

Keira stopped her search abruptly and looked up. The gentle glow of the porch light sparkled in her big brown eyes which were open wide; giving her an innocent and childlike appearance.

"Are you playing volleyball? Maybe I can come to your next game."

"Oh…uh…oh, found it, here's my key," she said dangling the Mickey Mouse key ring in front of his face as proof. It did not distract him from his question.

"Come on. I make a great cheerleader."

"No, I don't play volleyball. It's not like that. It's, um…" Keira struggled in search of an explanation. "It's piano lessons." She faked a quick smile and fidgeted nervously with her key. "No games, not even a recital, and I'm bad, really bad."

"Modest. That's something I didn't see coming."

The door swung open with a thud and inside stood an annoyed Nana. "Keira, it is almost midnight. Get inside now! Young man, you can see her at school on Monday. Good night."

Keira raised one eyebrow.

William extended his hand. "Ma'am, it's nice to meet you. I'm Will…"

"On Monday…" Nana interrupted. She put an arm around Keira and swept her inside. Keira got a quick "good night" out before Nana shut the door.

"Sweet dreams, Keira," William's muffled voice came from behind the front door. Then she heard his footsteps grow quieter, the bang of the pickup door closing, and finally the thunderous revving of his truck's engine as he zoomed away.

"Wow," Keira sighed as she glided to the couch.

"Cutting it awfully close, aren't we?"

"Midnight is still two whole minutes away."

"That's not the point."

"Did you hear him say 'sweet dreams'? How cute is that?"

Nana couldn't help but laugh at her goofy, love struck teenager. "Just be mindful of the time. That's all I ask. After all, tonight might be the night."

Of course it wasn't. Not yet.

The next morning, Keira was up at 5 a.m. to start her day. She worked with Nana non-stop. By 5 p.m. she was spent. After a long soak in the tub, she slipped into her pajamas early. They were her favorites, made of soft and warm blue flannel and dotted with penguins carrying presents. Of course, it was only autumn, too early for Christmas pajamas, but Keira didn't care. She loved these so much that she wore them year round. She was curled up in the big chair in front of the T.V. when there was a knock at the front door.

"Can you answer it?" she yelled in vain. As soon as the words passed her lips, she remembered that Nana had slipped out to pick up a few groceries. With a grunt, she got up and pulled the door open.

"Sexy jammies," William grinned.

Keira grinned too. "Thanks, they're penguins."

"Hello again, Mr. Swift." Nana appeared behind Keira, startling her so much that she jumped and her heart pounded. "Would you like to come in?"

William hesitantly stepped inside. He kept his hands in his pockets and spoke uneasily. "I knew that you said you were busy today, but I just thought I'd stop by anyway in case your plans changed."

"Oh, I've had a really hard day." She could see that he looked a little disappointed. That look was the last thing she wanted. "I was just watching some T.V., do you want to stay and watch with me?"

"And you are welcome to stay for dinner," Nana added.

"Sure," he said. Keira could keep from grinning as she led him to the den. He sat down on the sofa and she curled in beside him. Nana went straight to the kitchen to put away the groceries she had left there.

The couple spent the next few hours talking about anything and everything. Keira had been physically attracted to him before, but now she was beginning to think it could be much more.

He liked the same things. He even understood what it was like to be under pressure, what it was like trying to live up to everyone's expectations, and what it felt like to have your life mapped out for you. When she talked to Colby, he would listen and then distract her from what she was feeling. It wasn't like that with William. He listened to her on a whole new level. He could empathize with her. His life was very similar. Of course, his pressures were nothing compared to the ones she faced; but when they talked, she could tell that he really got it, even though she couldn't tell him everything.

William knew that she was holding something back, but he didn't care. He went out with her because he was told to do so. He never really expected it to turn into anything. Yet, he had felt something during that first date. He couldn't stop thinking about it.

That's what led him to Keira's house this night. The longer they talked, the more she confirmed it for him. There was something good, strong, and undeniable between them. He was absolutely falling in love with her. For the first time in his life, he was free. Free to live his life outside of expectations and destiny. With her, he felt hope.

Chapter 5: Fall Ball

"I have the best idea ever!"

Words more menacing had never before been spoken.

"Ever!" Brooke exclaimed. Ann and Keira knew it had to mean trouble. And it did. Brooke decided to share her cosmetic genius (her own words) to help her Coco Bear's friends get ready for the dance. Ann and Keira were less than thrilled with the invitation, but eagerly accepted once Colby became desperate enough to extend them free license to also call him "Coco Bear" anywhere and anytime they pleased.

On the day of the Fall Ball, Nana dropped Keira and Ann off in front of Brooke's house. In actuality, it was more of an estate, than a house. The paved circular drive rolled around a water fountain, complete with an angry statue of Poseidon which reigned by terror over the lawn.

Before Brooke's family moved in, the home was owned by a single, wealthy businessman who used it as a summer escape from the hustle and bustle of the big city. So, it had all the charm of a vacation getaway with all the conveniences of a metropolitan penthouse suite.

When the car stopped, Keira and Ann thanked Nana for the ride and gathered up their belongings. It was early afternoon, giving them plenty of time to goof off before getting ready. Keira slung her garment bag over her shoulder and hopped up the stone steps to press the intercom call button at the door.

"Banes residence, whom may I say is calling?" said an old, male voice.

"We're here to see Brooke," Keira replied.

"I see. Whom may I say is calling?"

The girls chuckled. "Keira Ryan and Ann Martin?"

"Very well."

The intimidating nine-foot arched double doors opened to a two-story foyer with marble floors and a gleaming crystal chandelier.

"Welcome ladies," said the butler.

They jumped. Neither of them had even realized that he was there until he spoke. The view was simply too distracting.

"Miss Banes will be ready to receive you shortly. She has asked that you wait in her bedroom. You will find it upstairs, four doors to the right. It is the white room." And with that he turned on the spot and was gone.

Keira and Ann stood in amazement. Neither of them had ever been in such an opulent home before. Despite Mrs. Banes' preference for modern fashion and design, all of the furnishings were antique. The wood was intricately carved and the silver was polished to a flawless shine. They made their way up the grand, spiraling staircase. At the top, they followed the butler's directions to the fourth door on the right.

"Do you think this is the right one?" Ann asked.

"I don't think they'll kick us out if we're wrong," Keira shrugged as she turned the knob.

They soon realized why the butler called it the white room. Every object within it was pristine white. Long, white, flowing sheers adorned the elongated windows. The high bed was piled with a white duvet and tons of pillows, shaded by a shimmering white canopy. The floor was even carpeted in a luscious white. Keira strode in and set her stuff on a fainting couch in the corner. Ann pulled off her shoes and delicately followed.

"Huh."

"Yeah."

"It's really white, isn't it?"

"Like a Yeti's butt!" Keira smirked.

Brooke appeared from a door on the far side of the room.

"Great, you're here. Let's get started. I'm so excited. Come on!" she invited the two to follow. She ducked back through the door with Ann and Keira behind. The door led to a cavernous closet and bathroom. The two girls couldn't help but think that their deal with Colby had worked out better than they could have ever anticipated.

They spent the entire afternoon together giggling, gossiping, and exploring Brooke's closet. As the starry night sky began to blanket the town, the ladies slipped into their evening gowns.

Brooke selected a sophisticated, fitted, black satin gown with matching stiletto heels. She wore a dazzling emerald necklace, worthy of any red carpet event. The stones brought out her eyes and made them almost glow. Her professionally styled hair was pulled up in a faultless French twist.

When the phone rang, Brooke had just put the finishing touches on Ann's hair, a chin-length meticulous bounty of tiny, spiraling dark red curls that glistened with glittered highlights. She answered the phone, "Coco Bear!". Her excitement quickly turned to dismay. He was going to be late. This news didn't score any points with Brooke. While she was pouting, Keira helped Ann into her dress, a shocking purple number, which perfectly matched her newly painted fingernails.

When Ann was ready, she helped Keira, who had chosen a daring, yet elegant, crimson gown. Her raven hair cascaded down her back in loose curls. Brooke had allowed Keira to do her own makeup since they were running out of time. She barely used any, just the eyes, a smidge of lipstick and her lingering summer tan. As a finishing touch, Brooke latched Keira's necklace for her. It was a delicate ruby teardrop that came with matching earrings. Nana had surprised her with them that morning.

The ladies peeked through the curtains excitedly as each guy arrived. First was Jumper who shocked everyone, but Ann, in a Hawaiian-print tie and cummerbund. Next was William who looked amazing in a traditional black tuxedo with a white shirt, black bow tie and vest. As he flashed his pearly whites, Keira couldn't help but think that he looked like some sort of a prince or movie star.

Everyone took a seat on the sofas of the formal living room while they waited. Ann took a few pictures and Jumper rehashed his tuxedo shopping adventures. As Colby's dad pulled in the drive, Brooke moved to the top of the stairs to make her grand entrance. Ann joked that Brooke had seen too many teen-princess-making-a-slow-motion-entrance movies.

"Get the door," Brooke fussed.

"It's your door," Keira answered as the others chuckled. "Where's a butler when you need one?"

"Oh, just let him in."

Keira gave William a quick kiss on the cheek and twisted out of his arms and off the sofa. She pulled open the large arched double doors. There stood Colby. He wore a sleek, black tuxedo, with monochrome black shirt, vest, and tie. Keira was surprised at first. She had, for no particular reason, anticipated that he would wear white. After all, doesn't the good guy always wear white?

The light from the front porch bounced off his golden hair and his knowing, blue eyes sparkled. Keira froze in disbelief at the sight. He didn't look like Coco Bear, nor did he look like her clumsy best friend. She was absolutely stunned. One corner of his mouth turned up slightly smirking. He leaned in to her. The closeness warmed her and she gasped for breath as his lips touched her ear.

"Keira, I think you're blocking Brooke's big entrance. Better move aside before she thinks you're trying to steal her thunder," he whispered.

"Oh," Keira mumbled with a half yes, half okay, and stepped clumsily behind him to close the door. Brooke glided down the stairs with a practiced elegance. As she reached the bottom, Colby took her hand and kissed it.

"We look so hot! We are so going to be the talk of the ball," Brooke squealed. "Let's go."

Brooke led the way as the group headed outside to the limousine that her father had taken the liberty to hire...anything for his princess. Colby lagged behind the group, eager to burn this image of friends and youth into his memory. But as he did this, he found his mind straying back to that last day of summer. Keira's dress was as brilliant as that magnificent sunset, flowing with every step she took. He shook his head to release the daydream in which he had accidentally wandered. Then another vision of her entered his head. It was Keira in her usual jeans and a hoodie. She pulled something from her sleeve. It was shiny...a knife. He watched as she pushed it into a man dressed in black.

"What are you doing? We're gonna be late," Brooke whined.

He faltered into the car, lightly bumping his head on the roof, and they were on their way.

The night was their own. Nearly the whole student population flocked to the windows to see who would emerge from the limo. Brooke was right, even as freshmen, they were the talk of the ball. Ann even convinced the D.J. to let Jumper have a try at the controls. After five dance mixes straight, he signed off with a slow number. Jumper led Ann to the dance floor and swept her across it into a not-so-graceful dip. Brooke took the opportunity to cool off and check her makeup in the restroom. William headed to find drinks, leaving Colby and Keira alone.

"Having fun?" Keira asked him.

He shook his head. "Sorry, I've got something on my mind."

"What's up?"

"I warn you. This is going to sound ridiculous. Umm, have you ever stabbed anyone before?"

Keira laughed.

"Okay, nevermind. I've just got a weird feeling. Promise me that you won't go anywhere by yourself?"

"Will do and speaking of not being alone, you and Brooke look pretty cozy."

"I know. I still can't believe she's with *me*."

The untold truth was that Colby's good looks were the only thing that kept him from truly being marked as a nerd. He certainly had the grades, coordination, and the attitude for it. Keira knew that he viewed himself that way. Still, she was surprised by his reaction to Brooke's attention.

"You really do like her, don't you?"

"Well, she's no William Swift, but I think I'll take her," he grinned past her.

William wrapped his muscular arms around Keira from behind. "Let's dance."

He moved his arms to twirl her around so that they were face to face. He placed one hand on the small of her back and pulled her close. Together they moved gracefully across the dance floor. They looked good as a couple. He was so agile that she wondered if he had taken dance classes. She had heard that some guys took ballet to help them with football. She'd also heard that some took it to meet girls. She hoped that William fell into the first category.

"Are you okay?" he asked. He noticed that her normal mischievous air had changed to a thoughtful expression.

She looked into his eyes. He smiled and did that thing he does when he takes a shy look at the ground. "Everything is right," she whispered in his ear.

The six danced, laughed, and when it was time to go home, their very own driver was waiting. Ann was the first to be dropped off at home. William was crashing at Jumper's house so they were next. As soon as William shut the car door, Keira transformed into a hyper, neurotic mess.

"It was great. Don't you think it went great? He's great. Isn't he? We have so much in common even though he's a junior and I'm just a freshman. He said he liked my shoes and did you see when he opened the door for me? He's perfect. I just want to be with him all the time, know what I mean?" she said in one, sustained breath. She finally inhaled and sunk into her seat, before continuing the constant stream of giddy babbling.

Colby and Brooke were relieved when the car stopped in Keira's driveway. She thanked Brooke for the ride and proceeded into the house.

"Whoa, is she always like that?"

"She's just hyped about this guy. She usually plays it very cool," Colby explained.

"I guess I understand that. He is so way out of her league."

"What?"

"I know that she's your friend, but really, Colby, I just don't think she's good enough for him."

"Why would you say that? Do *you* have a thing for William?"

"Trust me, he's so not my type," she snorted. She scooted closer to Colby and held his hand. "I'm sorry Coco Bear, you're right. I bet she was just annoying because of her nerves. You know that's probably also why she said that weird thing today."

"What do you mean?" asked Colby. He wasn't really interested, but didn't want to seem impolite. He put his arm around Brooke to show that he wasn't mad; but instead of looking at her, he looked up through the car's skylight to see the moon.

"She was going on and on about how tired she was and how she couldn't sleep," began Brooke. "Then she said the strangest thing. She said that if those stupid mogdocs didn't get her, the training would. Is she running the marathon or something?"

"Marathon? Keira? No way."

There it was again. He had heard that word before but couldn't place it. He was stuck on that word…mogdoc. "What's a mogdoc? I've heard that word somewhere before."

Brooke just sat there looking at him as if he had grown an arm out of the top of his head. "Oh, I think it's some kind of generic-brand clog," she answered dismissively. "You don't think that she's running a marathon in clogs? No wonder she's so tired."

"What?" Colby was stunned by Brooke's daft conclusion.

"Oh yeah, as soon as she said it, she tried to take it back…told me that was not what she said…that I had too much hair spray in my ears! I know what's what. I could tell right away that she didn't mean to say it. It just slipped out. Ann was in the bathroom, but I definitely heard it."

"It's probably nothing," he lied as he opened the car door. "But I'll be sure to look after her. Good night."

"You always protect her, don't you?"

"Yeah, it's kind of like a full time job, but who else is going to do it?"

She reached up and ran her fingers in his hair. He turned his head to her. She leaned in close and he suddenly found it harder to leave.

"Good night, Coco Bear."

Chapter 6: Halloween Bash

The leaves were soon changing color and a chill tinged the air. It was October and Jumper started making plans for his annual Halloween Bash. Of course, Jumper was a normal teenage boy. 'Making plans' to him meant finding a field, building a bonfire, and finding some girls to bring food and drinks.

This was simply not acceptable to Ann. She decided the make the Halloween Bash her new project. It was now a costume party, held in the ballroom of a creepy, abandoned hotel in the historic district. Ownership of the hotel had reverted to the town, and with his being a major election year and days before the polls were to open, it was easy to convince officials to allow free use of it to provide a safe, teen event. The place had been the source of many legendary ghost stories, which made it the perfect location for a Halloween party. Ann even got the parents to pitch in so she could buy food and book, *Sweet Kick*, a hot, local garage band.

By nine o'clock the party was already in high gear. Ann greeted Keira and William at the door when they arrived. William was dressed as a modern vampire. He looked sizzling, but Ann's eyes were fixed on his date. It actually took her a moment to realize it was her friend. Keira took one bubble gum pink fingernail and pushed back a strand of her blond wig. She wasn't used to wearing dresses, especially ones this short. She gave it a tug and fussed with the big silver cross around her neck.

"Let me guess, you're coming to the party as Brooke?" Ann joked.

"I'm supposed to be Buffy the Vampire Slayer, but now that I think about it…"

The two laughed.

"What are you? Cowboy? Pirate?" Keira asked. Ann was wearing brown pants and boots with a white shirt and brown leather vest.

"I wish."

Jumper surprised her from behind with drinks in his hands.

"Oh, I get it," Keira looked over the couple. "Lovely, you are, pretty, pretty," she said with her very best Yoda impression. Jumper had convinced Ann to dress up as Han Solo to compliment *his* Princess Leia costume.

"Nice mask, Ryan, very scary," Jumper grinned. Of course Keira wasn't wearing a mask. "Actually you look kinda hot tonight, you know, nothing like your usual self."

Before she could respond, he put down the cups and turned to Ann, "Help me Ann Solo, you're my only hope…to get my dance on! Come on, babe. Let's show these losers some real moves."

"Sounds like a challenge to me," William laughed and they followed their friends up the creaky stairs to the ballroom.

The ballroom was packed. Ann had thought of everything. Black satin drapes reached from the floor to the twelve foot ceiling behind a temporary stage which was built on the end of the long ballroom. Laser lights beamed across the ceiling and the band's amps were blasting. Colby and Brooke were already in front of the stage. Colby, the knight in shining armor, had his hands at the waist of his overly-done pink princess.

"Of course she's a princess," mumbled Keira.

"Princess?" William looked up to see what Keira was talking about then chuckled, "Yeah, the little princess always has to be the center of attention."

"You noticed that too?"

Brooke was certainly over-the-top this time. Keira could see that Colby even wore a big, emerald medallion on his costume, an obvious addition from his girlfriend.

Brooke and Colby were completely focused on the band, jumping and singing along. The fun they were having was contagious and soon Ann, Jumper, William, and Keira were dancing along too. Unfortunately, their good time was coming to a screeching halt.

About halfway into *Sweet Kick*'s second set, a scream rang out. "Stay here with the girls," Colby directed William. He nodded and took a protective stance in front of Keira. Brooke rolled her eyes and Colby could hear her grumbling about protecting herself as he leapt into action.

Colby and Jumper dodged through the startled crowd and jumped over a couple of chairs to get to the heart of the commotion. A sophomore girl, dressed as a witch, was standing on a barstool crying and pointing. "There's something under here. It grabbed my leg."

"What'd it look like?"

"It's about the size of a raccoon, a little bigger maybe, but much...much ickier. I'm not getting off this chair!"

"I don't see anything. Colby, can you see behind the bar?"

"Yeah and it's all clear."

"Come on, Shara," her friends urged.

"I...AM....NOT...GETTING...OFF...THIS ...CHAIR!"

Tears streamed down her face and her hands shook uncontrollably. However, by the end of the song, after tons of coaxing, she timidly eased off the stool and hurried down the stairs with her friends in tow.

"What do you suppose that was all about?" Colby asked Jumper.

"She probably just got freaked out. This old place is starting to get to me too. I was back in the kitchen a little while ago and I could have sworn that I felt someone brush past me, but when I turned to look, no one was there."

Not a second after he spoke, more screams rang out. This time they were coming from the opposite side of the room. Ann's shriek was the loudest.

"Ann!" Jumper bellowed. He and Colby looked at each other and dashed back to the stage. The area in front of the stage had cleared and the band stopped abruptly. Ann was on top of a chair. William had grabbed up Keira, and despite her outrage, was carrying her like a sack of potatoes. Brooke stood in the center of the drama, her arms folded, with a look like she was bored out of her mind.

People started pouring out of the room and down the stairs to the front door. Some thought it was a practical joke, some thought it was real ghosts, but the most common explanation was a rat. Everyone was okay. Regardless, within minutes, only the six remained plus the two youngest members of the band who were charged with packing up the instruments.

The guys decided to sweep the floors and look for signs of the intruder. They found nothing. As soon as they finished, Colby headed home to study for Monday's geometry exam, but Brooke decided to stay and help as the girls tore down decorations and packed up the leftover food. An hour later, the remaining band members headed out and the last streamer found its way to the trash can.

The gang gathered at the bar in the back of the ballroom to take a break and talk.

"Did you see that animal?" William asked.

"No," said Keira. "You saw it, didn't you, Ann?"

"I heard it, but it was too quick. I didn't get a look at it."

Jumper added, "That science girl, Shara, was the first to see it."

"Science girl?" Ann and Keira asked together.

"Oh," Ann realized Jumper's rationale and explained. "She won the science fair last week with her additive that speeds up the composting process." Ann had written an article on it for the school paper.

"I didn't see Shara. What was she dressed as?" Keira asked.

"She was a witch."

"Noticed her, did you?" Ann raised a brow at Jumper.

"Of course I did, she had the same huge necklace that our boy was wearin'," he replied pointing to Brooke. "It's kind of hard to miss."

"Oh." Brooke glared at him. "It's not a necklace, it's a medieval medallion. Colby was dressed as a knight and they wore things like that back then."

"Whatever helps you sleep at night," William rolled his eyes at Brooke and sighed. "Anyway, whatever it was, it isn't here now. It was probably just a squirrel and got scared away by all the screaming."

"I'm sure you're right," Brooke agreed as Ann's phone rang.

"No way! Yeah, I know her. She was just here. Okay Dad, we're fine. We'll lock the doors and stay here until you arrive. Hurry, Keira's supposed to be home before midnight," she said.

"What's up?" Keira asked.

"That was my Dad. He said that a kid from our school is missing."

Keira's stomach knotted. He shouldn't have left early. She should have gone with him to make sure he made it home okay. She looked at Ann, her gaze giving her away, but she wasn't the first to speak up.

"It's Colby, isn't it?" Brooke chimed in.

Ann scrambled, "No, no, it's not Colby. It's…"

"Shara," Jumper guessed.

"Yeah, can you believe it? Oh, here it is."

"Are you sure?" Brooke asked.

Her phone beeped with an incoming text. She rose to show them the message, an amber alert for Shara Nelson last seen forced into a black van by a caucasian male.

"Can you believe this? We were just talking about her. I hope she's okay," Ann said shaking her head.

"Maybe it's the same guy that took Bobby," Jumper chimed in. Everyone looked at him questioningly. "You know they finally tracked down that bum. The one that everyone thought took Bobby at the skate park. Well, he didn't. They found his body in a freezer at a deserted crack house in Virginia. He O.D.'d two days before Bobby was taken. There's no way he did it, so the police are back to square one."

"Anyway, Dad said that he's coming to pick us up. He wants us to lock the doors until he gets here. I think it's a good idea. Guys, can you get the front door? I'll head to the back," Ann said. Jumper headed to the door as William pulled Keira aside.

"Are you okay?" He stroked her cheek.

"I'm totally fine, just a few goose bumps." She pressed her hand against his as he held it on her cheek.

William breathed a sigh of relief. "You're amazing. Nothing shakes you," he smiled and did that shy look to the ground thing that he does. "I couldn't imagine what I would have done if you got hurt tonight. You know that I really care about you."

"I know. I care about you too."

He pulled her close and kissed her forehead. "You know, I wasn't sure about asking you out; I mean, the first time, at the pep assembly. Really, I was kind of pushed into it."

She wrinkled her forehead. He laughed, "No, it's not what you think. I'm just trying to say that I'm really glad that I did. Now, I can't imagine being apart from you." He nuzzled her neck. She could smell his cool cologne and felt her heartbeat speed up.

"Hey, hey, break it up," Jumper ordered. Keira glared at him.

As if it were on cue, they heard Ann's father knocking on the door. Ten minutes later, William said goodbye and thundered away in his red pickup, as the rest tumbled into the Martin family minivan.

Chapter 7: The Unusual Suspect

The next few weeks were pretty uneventful for the gang. There was still no news about Shara or Bobby.

The first of December was an unusually warm Saturday. An unusually warm December day in southern Ohio still means heavy jacket, hat, and boots; yet, William and Keira dragged everyone outside for Christmas caroling. Jumper was the only one who got out of it. He had a terrible cold, at least that's what he told William.

Everyone fit snuggly in William's extended cab Ford as they made their way into town. They parked near the post office. The guys straggled behind silently as the girls strolled arm in arm down the sidewalk ahead. Their off-key carols got louder and louder until giggles finally overtook them. They were rounding the corner of Park and Court when a squad car pulled up with lights ablaze. Two officers emerged from the car. Colby recognized the youngest uniformed officer, but it was the older policeman that spoke first.

"Are you Colby Hayes?"

"Yes, officer…sir, what's going on?"

"Son, we need you to come with us to the police station. Your parents are already waiting for us there. We need to ask you a few questions."

"Smitty, are you arresting me?" he pleaded.

The younger officer, Officer Ben Smith, known to locals simply as Smitty, was seven years older than Colby. He was the same age as Colby's brother, Jamie. Colby could remember Jamie and Smitty spending many long, Saturday afternoons camped out in front of the T.V. to watch the Ohio State Buckeyes play. It was this connection that forced Smitty to step in. "Colby, we just need to ask you a few questions about those kids that were taken."

"You think he's involved?" Keira asked as she moved in front of Colby.

"Miss, just move on, please. We'll take care of this."

"That's the most ridiculous thing I've ever heard. He didn't even know Bobby."

"Keira, I *do* know Bobby. I was tutoring him in chemistry," Colby admitted. "But, I was in the lab, prepping for my advanced chemistry placement test on the day he disappeared. I'm sure the school has a sign-in sheet or something."

"Yeah, that's right and he was with us when Shara disappeared. We were all together, cleaning up after our Halloween party," she added.

Colby looked at her with warning in his eyes. Ann and William dropped their gaze to the sidewalk.

"Mr. Hayes, I have to advise you to stop talking. This matter should only be discussed with your parents present. Come with us," the older officer insisted.

He nodded and followed Smitty to the back door of the squad car. Smitty gently shut the door and quickly slipped into the passenger's seat. The senior officer gave a satisfied nod and issued a fatherly warning of "keep your noses clean" to the others, before ducking into the car himself. They zoomed away.

No one really felt like singing anymore. They began to quietly stroll down the street to the post office where William had parked the truck. Well, quietly, except for Keira. She was infuriated by the policemen's visit and let everyone know it. Once at the truck, Brooke announced that she was meeting her Dad at the pharmacy next door. Without even a goodbye, she darted away.

Ann opened the door and then the half door to the extended cab back seat and slipped inside. She shut the doors quickly to keep the cold air out. Keira and William stood outside for a moment. Keira was still fuming. William tried to calm her down. He took her hands and leaned in close.

"Keira, I love you. You've got to calm down. Why are you so upset? They're just going to ask him a few questions."

She threw out her arms breaking his grip. He fell back a few steps from the force. Her strength surprised him. She was strong, very strong. He stepped back and looked at her. William knew that she hadn't meant to hurt him when she pushed him away. He flexed his fingers and rubbed his wrist. "I can't believe it," he muttered, shaking his head in doubt.

Hurt and angry, he turned from her and climbed into the truck. Keira took a long, calming breath and took her place in the passenger seat. She felt the rush of hot air from the dashboard. She closed her eyes and let the soothing warmth flow over her. It felt good, but it didn't help her mood.

"I can't believe Brooke. She didn't even speak up when the police carried her boyfriend away," Ann noted.

"She certainly didn't waste any time getting out of here," William noted.

"She probably had to rush home to take a shower. She's dating an ex-con now."

"I don't want to hear this," Keira snapped with her eyes still closed and her forehead wrinkled with stress.

William couldn't take it any longer. "Keira, why on earth did you do that?"

Her eyes burst open. "Do what? Stick up for my friend? It was more than Brooke did."

"It was the police. It's not like a bully stole his lunch money."

"I had to do it. I know he didn't do this."

"You LIED to the police. He left the party before Shara was snatched and you know it. He didn't even have a good excuse, just something lame about studying."

Ann fell silent in the back seat and suddenly wished she could disappear without being noticed.

"I protected my friend. I don't regret it. End of subject."

"Yeah, you protected him, like you always do. I suppose it's your duty to protect him."

"What are you talking about? The only problem here, William, is your sudden, insane jealousy."

"No, the problem is that I love you and you've been lying to me this whole time," William said. "I can't believe it," he muttered under his breath, massaging one of his hurting wrists.

"Calm down guys," Ann intervened. "We were only kidding. You know Colby. He's squeaky clean. I bet he's already home."

William fumed as he slammed the gas pedal and the engine roared. Even though it was out of his way to do so, he dropped Keira off first.

"I'm home," she yelled as she darted for her bedroom. She plopped on the bed and texted Colby. There was no reply.

Looking for a distraction, she decided to head to the kitchen and help Nana with dinner. It helped her mood to see that it was her favorite, lasagna and garlic bread. She was enjoying her meal in silence, hoping that Nana wouldn't ask about the day's events, when the phone rang.

"Just sit there and finish eating. I'll get it."

"Thank you, sweetheart," Nana said.

Keira answered it before the second ring. To her relief, it was Colby. She took the cordless handset to her room, hopefully out of reach for Nana's extremely keen sense of hearing.

"Hey."

"What happened? Tell me everything."

"Not much to tell. They asked me where I was when Bobby and Shara disappeared. I told them the same thing that we told the police when they pulled up. Mom and Dad didn't really remember when I got home, so they assumed that I helped with the party clean up. It's something I would normally do and I've never given them a reason not to believe me."

Colby took in a deep breath and asked, "Did Brooke say anything about it?"

"This isn't about Brooke."

"It's just that I tried to call, but there's no answer. Do you think she's screening my calls? She must have been so embarrassed. Do you think she'll ever talk to me again?"

Keira started to argue that not everything was about Brooke, but knew that she needed to put her irritation in check and attempt to relieve his concern. After all, she was his best friend and this was probably one of the worst days of his life.

"Brooke's not going to break up with you for this," she said calmly. "She's not ignoring you, she's not even home. She was running errands with her Dad this evening, probably forgot her phone or let the battery run down. So, you have nothing to worry about."

"Good," he said. An awkward silence followed. Colby couldn't stop worrying about Brooke. Keira couldn't think of anything else to say that wouldn't make her seem jealous or insensitive.

"By the way, I've got to say thanks for stepping in, but you shouldn't have," Colby managed.

"You know that I can't stand to lie and you could have been caught."

"You were in trouble, so I couldn't help myself. You sound just like William. He was furious with me, he said he loved me and he wanted me to calm down."

The words no more than left her lips when she realized it. "Oh no, he said he loved me. I didn't even catch it. I pushed him away. I mean, literally, I physically pushed him away."

"Wow that *is* bad."

"Yeah, tell me about it. I think he may have said it more than once."

"Do you love him?"

Her chest tightened as she thought about how angry William was with her. "Let's just forget about William and me for now. I want to talk about why the police were questioning you."

Colby spoke carefully, "Well, Bobby and Shara ran in two very different social circles, but I was tutoring Bobby and Shara and I shared lab time before the science fair, so I was a common factor in both of their lives."

"So, they think the two disappearances are connected?"

"Sounds like it. They said that there were the same muddy footprints at each scene."

"I'm just glad you're okay."

"For now, but I feel like I have to get to the bottom of this thing. My alibis aren't rock solid. They could come after me again."

"Footprints are all they have to go on?" she asked.

"That's pretty much it. So, they're trying to find suspects through commonalities. That's how they found me."

"So," Keira pondered. "What about their parents, any ties there?"

"Worlds apart, just like their kids. Bobby's parents are divorced. His mom works at an art gallery in San Diego, a real free spirit type. He lives here with his Dad who owns a nightclub in Grant. Shara's parents are doctors at St. Joseph's."

"Dead end there," she said. "What about siblings?"

"Nope. Both are the only child in their family."

"That could be something."

"I don't see how, but I suppose it could," Colby mumbled in exasperation. "Listen, I've had a long day. I'm taking a shower and going to bed. Talk to you tomorrow?"

"Sure," she replied absentmindedly, still deeply immersed in thought.

"Keira, you know that I didn't do this, right?"

"I have no doubt."

Chapter 8: Christmas Break

The last day of school before Christmas break seemed to last an eternity. The whole gang ate lunch together in the commons and finalized their plans for some Christmas shopping at the mall after school. William could only fit five in his extended cab pickup, so Brooke said she would just meet them there. Those that were riding with William decided to meet at the fountain right after the last bell. The mall was an hour's drive each way, so timing was important.

Classes were simple since no new lessons could be started. The holidays were on everyone's minds. Keira sat in her last class, with her arms folded on her desk as she stared at the clock's hands. Jumper and Ann held hands between their desks as the elderly Mrs. Cannon hummed *Silent Night* and handed out graded economics term papers. William started an impromptu three-on-three basketball game in the final minutes of gym class. Brooke was in the bathroom, refreshing her hair and touching up her lips with candy cane lip gloss. Colby finished writing his Christmas break reading list.

Finally the bell rang. A simultaneous "Yes!" rang out from the entire student body and faculty. The classrooms emptied into the hall. The crowd moved quickly outside and spread like lava leaking from an active volcano. In the student parking lot, car radios blared and horns honked marking the mass exodus to freedom.

Ann, William, and Colby were the first to arrive at the fountain. Ann pulled on her gloves as William buttoned up his letterman jacket. Colby, outfitted in a parka appropriate for an Alaskan expedition, paced back and forth in front of the group. Jumper arrived shortly after William fastened his last button. He met Ann with a quick kiss. Lastly, as always, Keira arrived. She twirled and leisurely bounced down the school steps toward her friends. Her face was glowing with the freedom of Christmas break.

Without so much as a glance at Keira, William ordered, "Let's head out." Being the only one with a driver's license, William took the leadership role when it came to activities outside school. Today, he seemed more annoyed than usual by Keira's inability to stick to the schedule. They would now be at the back of the pack fleeing from the student parking lot.

Still, they made good time and arrived in just under an hour. Once inside the mall's food court, they met up with Brooke, completed their game plan and split up. Brooke and Colby headed to the anchor department store to look for a sweater and purse for Colby's grandmother and a toy for his nephew. Ann and Jumper rode the escalator down to the jewelry store to get something flashy for her mother. Keira and William decided to head to the two-story music store for some browsing and holiday sales. The group decided to meet back in the food court at eight.

Brooke and Colby were two very determined people. Hand in hand, they quickly made their way out of sight. Ann and Jumper strode off, giggling, teasing each other about getting their feet caught in the escalator. That left Keira and William alone. They strolled slowly past the glittering storefronts, occasionally taking a moment to stop and gaze at a display.

Keira was particularly amazed by the display at a store called The Wheel, a wine and cheese shop. The window was dressed as the interior of an Old World vineyard main house on Christmas Eve. Dozens of tiny, mechanically-animated mice, outfitted in red and green scarves, hats, and mittens were cavorting among the wine barrels and cheese wheels. She spotted one skipping atop a wheel of cheddar cheese. Another was swinging on a garland of pine and holly. Six were ice skating on a frozen puddle of chardonnay from a knocked over bottle. There was even a little girl and boy mouse under the mistletoe. She could have stared at it for hours, but for some reason the display only seemed to make William more irritated. Before she knew it, he had wandered away. Keira ran a few steps to catch up. As she reached his side, they found themselves at the entrance to the music store.

"Is this where you wanted to go?" William asked looking at his watch impatiently.

"We don't have to...I just thought..."

"Whatever."

This mood was not acceptable to Keira. She resolved to cheer him up fast. Keira grabbed his collar with both hands and pulled him close enough that their noses touched. "What would you like for Christmas, little boy?" she asked suggestively.

"Stop it," he said as he broke her grip and stepped back. "You know, I have other things that I could be doing right now."

"Don't let me keep you."

"I didn't mean...I just...You make me so..." he broke off. He did that shy thing where he shakes his head and looks at the ground.

"Don't do that. Out with it."

"Fine," he said. "I'm done."

"Okay, let's go in the store then."

"No," William stopped. "I didn't want it to be like this, but I'm done. I can't do this anymore. I'm done with us."

"Did I do something?"

"There are just too many secrets."

"My secrets? I've never even been to your house."

"What are you always training for? You're getting stronger and faster, that's not due to piano lessons. I've never even seen a piano in your house. And what's with the whole Cinderella routine every night at midnight?"

"That's nothing."

"Oh yeah, and why did you tell the police that Colby was with us after the Halloween party."

She shook her head. "I thought you were over that."

"It's just that you're a…a…," he couldn't seem to get the words out. He wouldn't let himself say it, so he dug deep in search of something that would hurt. "You're just a freshman. You're still a child."

That was the last straw. Now, she was angry. "Why? Because I don't care about the consequences when it comes to protecting my friends?"

"I just can't believe that I didn't really know you. I've been so blind and stupid."

"That's just an excuse. William, you know me. You know that what's between us is real. I can't believe you're acting like this."

"No, I thought I knew you, but I didn't. Not really. And now the only thing that I'm sure of is that we can't be together."

"You have got to be kidding. Are you breaking up with me?"

"I think that I have to."

Keira's chin lowered for a fraction of a moment; then she held her head up high. "No strings. You want out, you're out." She turned on her heel and started into the store. She could hear William calling after, but he didn't follow. She hurried to the back of the store until she could no longer hear him.

As she rounded the last row of racks, she almost fell over a particularly perky-looking, pony-tailed store employee who had knelt down to restock some low shelves. Keira stopped within inches of the focused worker and pretended to thumb through some CDs.

The girl popped to her feet. Her extra-large "Suzie" name tag shown like a smiley billboard on her chest. "Can I help you find anything? I love this band too. They are so delicious, am I right? Did you see the new posters we have for them up front; they're buy one, get one," she sang.

Keira didn't even turn to look at her. She couldn't. She wouldn't. She was on the verge of tears and even something as slight as facing a human being would open the floodgates. She simply continued flipping through the CD jackets in silence.

After a few moments, Suzie shrugged and bounced to the next section where she spotted a confused-looking grandmother with a Christmas shopping list in hand. With the absence of Suzie's super-perky aura, Keira was able to compose herself. She pulled out her phone and dialed Colby's number.

Colby looked to see who it was before answering.

"No, Keira, I don't want a *Sweet Kick* poster for Christmas," he started without even a greeting.

Keira was startled. Did he see what happened? Was he in the store? As she debated this in her head, her silence lingered.

"Oh, didn't you go to the music store? I saw a bogo ad for the posters on the store window when we passed. I was sure that you were calling to tease me about it," he admitted.

"Guess I missed that one. That would have been hilarious. Anyway, listen, William is really sick. It just came on suddenly. I'm thinking that it may have been something from the Food Court," she lied. She told Colby that she was going to make sure William got home okay. Colby agreed and said that it would be no problem for the rest of them to find rides home later. Her voice was not its usual casual and teasing tone, but she was still convincing. She would not need to face her friends, at least not that evening. She ended the call and texted Nana for a ride home.

Chapter 9: The First Vox

Once at home, Keira went directly to her room. Nana followed behind. "Are you feeling okay?" she asked. "Tonight might be the night." Keira was growing weary of that phrase. Nana had repeated it every night over the last few months.

She turned to look at Nana's face. Even through the sincere concern, Keira picked up on a twinkle of excitement in her wise, hazel eyes.

"I'm fine, just tired," she replied and closed the bedroom door. However, Keira was not fine. She was devastated.

"Yeah right, like he was ever *my* sweet William. I'm such an idiot."

How could he talk to her like that? He thought that she was a child. Sure, it wasn't entirely his fault. She did have to lie to him, but he had no idea of the real Keira. He had no idea of her power. But then she realized that nobody did. Colby certainly didn't know, but again, he would never have treated her that way.

As the hours passed, she found herself wishing for the comfort of her friend. She had paced and paced, revisiting every word of the argument, thinking about what she should have said, what she should have done, and what she should have anticipated. The anxiety built up in the pit of her stomach until she could no longer bear it. Unstable and restless, she felt that she had to do something, anything. She couldn't sleep or distract herself from it. Grieving alone in silence was just not her way. She finally decided that the only remedy was immediate action. She had to do something now.

Keira quietly slipped on a jacket, sweatpants, and a pair of old tennis shoes that she found in the back of her closet. Even just the anticipation of action, seemed to lift her spirits. She opened the window and lowered herself out of it and onto the ground. This was one of the great benefits of living in a ranch-style home. She had broken out of her room so many times before, usually after being grounded. It felt easy and almost natural. She made her way through the corn field. The freezing winter wind cut her face and dried her lips. She quickly noticed that in her haste, she had forgotten socks. She was regretting that now, but not enough to turn back. Besides, the cold only made her move faster toward Colby's house.

Colby's room was at the top of the stairs in his family's two-story farmhouse. The residence was dark except for a forgotten porch light and a dim shimmer from Colby's room. Over the years, Keira had learned to navigate the rose trellis outside his window. She started up the wooden structure now, careful not to make too much noise. She reached the top and pushed the unlocked window open. Colby always left it unlocked for Keira. As she peeked in, she could see that the shimmer was coming from his laptop perched at the desk in the far corner. She was relieved to know that he was still awake.

"Geez. Shut the window. Were you born in a barn?" Colby whispered.

"Sorry," Keira forced the sash down and moved toward the light.

"What's up?"

"Nothing," she said. "I was just bored and..."

He looked up from his computer and directly into her eyes. "Right, like I would believe that you would walk a quarter of a mile in the middle of the freezing night and climb a rickety old trellis just to say 'hi'," he smirked. "I think I know you better than that."

"It's hardly a quarter mile."

She sat down on the edge of his bed. It, like the rest of Colby's room, was perfectly pristine. The familiarity eased her. Just being in his presence gave her immediate relief. It was as if his calm enveloped her, but she knew that the time to fess up was nearing. She scanned the walls, looking for a distraction.

He looked back down at the laptop. It was 11:59. He was tired. If he wanted to get some sleep before morning, he would need to give her a push.

Colby joined her on the corner of the bed. "All right, spill it."

The ball of anxiety in her gut was writhing now. She could no longer take it. She exploded. "William dumped me. He said he was 'done'. Can you believe it?" Keira was so upset that her voice shook with each word. "Did you see this coming?"

"No," Colby lied.

Unfortunately, she knew him too well and he wasn't a skilled liar. "I know what you're thinking, but I really liked him. It wasn't just a crush this time. I think I love him. It really hurts. It really, really hurts. I feel like I need to do something to fix this, but I don't know what. I don't think I can fix it."

She fell into Colby's chest sobbing. He put his arm around her. As he did, he felt a freezing wind rushing around them. He turned to see if the window had flown open. The wind was hard. Keira's long hair blew into his face. A blinding red light pierced his eyes. A sudden pressure on his chest knocked the breath from his lungs. "I've got you," Colby gasped.

"Let go!" she yelled, which only made him tighten his grip on her.

The biting cold took hold of them and pulled. Everything went black.

***

Colby gradually found his way back to consciousness. His head and chest were heavy. He tried to lift up, but could not budge. It was impossible to move. His muscles simply refused to react to the commands his brain was now screaming. He felt something soft against his face and realized that he was on the floor. The room was dark and his vision was heavily blurred.

"Help," he tried to yell, but no more than a huff left his lips. That's when he realized the most obvious detail. *This isn't my floor*, he thought. *This isn't MY bedroom!*

His face was buried in a pale, blue carpet. He managed to turn his head to one side and he scanned the dark room for Keira. She was standing over a wooden crib in the center of the room. A small, white light glowed from inside the baby bed. He blinked his eyes, trying to force himself awake. This couldn't be real.

He tried again to shout out to Keira. This time he mustered a low grunt. Keira raised her head at the sound. In a single movement, she reached down to her feet and turned. She spotted Colby and seemed surprised, but turned back to the crib and lifted an infant wrapped in a blanket from it. The soft light highlighted her black hair and made her appear dreamlike. She held the babe for a few moments, ignoring Colby's muted pleas for help. The white light dimmed. When the room was completely dark, she carefully placed the infant back into the crib and took a step backward.

Colby felt the wind again. He could see a nearby shelf lined with books, untouched by the force, standing perfectly still. Strange, but it seemed that this wind was centered on just him. No, it was centered on her. With a twirling motion, it picked up speed quickly.

Keira reached out to him. "Hurry, grab my hand!"

He drew enough strength to thrust his right hand toward her. She snatched it and pulled him to her with one hand. He draped his arms around her limply as he attempted to stand on his own. "You're okay, I've got you," she shouted to him as the wind started to pull on them. He focused his blurred eyes on her. Her face was absolutely glowing and her hair lifted into the vortex of the wind. The vibrant red light overtook them and everything went black…again.

***

This time Colby awoke in a place more familiar. He was on the ancient horsehair sofa in Keira's living room. Nana knelt beside him, dotting his forehead with a cool, damp cloth. "Are you awake, dear?" Nana asked. "That must have been some dream. I think that you got a touch of that food poisoning from the Food Court too."

"What?" Colby asked. He was shaken, but he still knew the difference between what he had just witnessed and a dream. "What's going on?" He pushed Nana's hand away. "Stay away from me."

He could see Keira lurking in the doorway. Nana put down the cloth and retreated to her. The two started arguing in hushed tones while Colby watched helplessly. He took those moments to assess his current predicament. He knew that he could not depend on his legs to carry him out the door. He knew that he had left his phone on his desk at home. His mind started racing, searching for a means of escape. This is completely insane, he thought. But, his survival instinct was now in full control. His head and his gut were screaming at him to run, but his body could not support the effort. He started breathing rapidly. His heart beat fast. And then everything went black for a third time.

He awoke this time to find that he hadn't moved. He was still on the antique couch in the living room at Keira's house. He felt rested and a bit calmer. He could also feel that his strength was returning. Yet, his head was throbbing. He held it in both hands and pressed on his temples in a feeble attempt to release the pain. He sat up with care and examined his surroundings. The room was silent, except for the unrelenting ticking of the grandfather clock in the corner. Nana and Keira were standing in the doorway between the room and the kitchen. He focused on them, still not able to stand of his own merit.

Colby could tell that they were having a heated conversation and that it was nearing an end. At last, Nana shook her head and threw up her arms. She left the doorway in the direction of the kitchen. Keira walked into the living room and sat on the coffee table beside the sofa. Her hands were clenched nervously.

"What have you done to me?"

The question took Keira aback. "What have I done to you?" Her brow furled, then an understanding smirk broke across her face. "Is that what you really think of me?," she said. "What do *you* think happened?"

"I can't. I'm not sure." His mind started to clear. He began to remember that this was his friend. He knew that there had to be a sensible explanation. He started thinking out loud, "A tornado?...but, the house is intact...was I hit in the head?" Colby couldn't piece it together. Nothing made sense and wasn't there something about a baby?

"Ooh...tornado...interesting, that's a new one, very clever," Keira noted. "Have you heard that one before?" she shouted toward the kitchen. Nana didn't answer. "Guess not," she shrugged.

Keira was eerily confident despite the unusual events of the evening. Her posture was very erect, not the slouched, easy-going stance that she usually exhibited. It was clear to Colby that she knew exactly what was going on and was even a bit pleased by it. It's her fault, he thought. She did do something to me, he thought. However, it was a fleeting notion. He couldn't bring himself to truly believe that she would ever hurt him. Still, Colby's head was pounding and he was in no mood for games. He planted his feet and quickly rose only to find that it was a little too quickly. He wobbled and Keira came to his support.

"Seriously, rest a little. You've been through a lot. I'll tell you everything you want to know. In fact, I can't wait to finally tell you everything," Keira reassured him. She eased him back onto the sofa. Her words soothed him, but the slowness of her delivery was taking its toll.

"Do you trust me, Colby?" Keira asked. "Are you my friend no matter what?"

His brief moment of relief now turned to concern. "Trust? You're talking to me about trust? Now? Just tell me what's going on," Colby demanded. Then he looked at her. He really looked at her, his best friend, seeking to confide in him. He took a deep, cleansing sigh. "Keira, you know that you can trust me. If you need help, I'm here." He started to feel that nervous twinge in his stomach, the same one that he got every time he knew Keira's exploits were going to get him into trouble.

"If *I* need help," she laughed. "You're the one who is flat on his back."

It didn't take long to see that Colby wasn't laughing. Fear consumed his face. She could see it now. She stifled the giggles and continued for his sake. "And you'll keep my secret? You must promise your most sacred promise to me."

"I guess we're in this together, like always."

"Good," she said. "Some of this will be very unbelievable, but I swear to you, it is true, I'll prove it to you." Colby could always tell when Keira was lying, another benefit of their long-time friendship. He knew that this was not one of those times.

"Tonight, you got to see something extremely rare. It was by accident, but I'm glad it happened," Keira said. Her tone was almost giddy.

"Glad? I feel like I've been run over by a truck and you're glad? What's going on? Did you do this?" Colby questioned. "What did I s..." his words dropped off as he saw what Keira was doing. Her eyes were closed. Her hands were cupped at her chest. From within them was the same tiny, white glowing light that he remembered from the nursery. He blinked his eyes to adjust them to the light. Startled, Colby drew his legs up and moved as far back on the sofa as possible.

Still he couldn't take his eyes from it. As he focused, he realized that it was not an orb like he expected. At its core it wasn't perfectly round, but more egg-shaped. The core itself didn't seem tangible, just a denser light than the outer part.

She opened her eyes and stared knowingly into his. "It's okay, Colby. This is a vox," she said calmly. "It's kinda like my gift." She closed her eyes again and the light slowly faded out as she pushed it against her chest.

"What is that? What are you?"

Keira's mouth fell open. She had tried to be calm and understanding for her friend, even though her insides were jumping at the excitement of telling him everything. This is all she'd ever dreamed of. She was just moments from confiding it all. How could he say that? It hit her like a swift kick to the stomach.

"What are you?"

His words repeated over and over in her head. Her first reaction was to cry, but crying is a gesture of weakness. Displays of weakness were simply not in Keira's nature, so instead, she turned that emotion to defense.

"I'm Keira. I'm the same Keira that's been your friend for as long as either of us can remember. I just have this one thing."

She was right. He knew that this was still his friend. He would struggle to remember that, for her sake. Colby could feel that what he had said hurt her and she was unsure whether to proceed with her explanation. Still, he had to know.

"I'm sorry. Go ahead. Please, I'm listening."

"Are you sure, Colby? There are things that you can't un-know."

He looked into her eyes and nodded.

She let out a gasp of exasperation and flopped on the floor beside him. She took a quick moment to compose herself.

"Okay, so here it is. I've practiced this in my head a bunch of times, so don't laugh."

"I promise you, I'm in no mood to laugh."

"Okay," she said, taking a deep breath. "In all the world, only a handful of people are meant for greatness. I don't mean politicians or those of blood nobility, I mean truly great people. They are those that change the course of history for the better. Some are known to man and famous for their work. Others are nobodies who by their actions start a ripple effect that changes the entire world," Keira said.

"So what does this have to do with anything?" Colby prodded. "Are you telling me that you are going to change the world?" Nothing was making sense to him and this just sounded like a lot of blah, blah, blah.

"Just listen." Keira continued, "When there is good, there is also evil. There are those that wish to stop the great ones from growing up to make their contribution to society. There are three times that this can be done. The times when they are most vulnerable, when they receive their vox," she said looking down at her hands.

"That glowing thing, the thing you were holding in the nursery?"

"Yes," Keira answered. "There are three vox bestowed to a great one by their guardian. The first vox is the Voice of Passion or you might say emotion, or maybe more accurately, devotion. It's given to the great one in infancy, right after they cut their first tooth."

She continued, "The second vox is the Voice of Truth. The great one receives it when he or she passes from infancy into childhood, signified by losing their first baby tooth. The third and most precious vox is the Voice of Wisdom, given at the sunset of childhood when their last baby tooth is lost. I am one of many who protect the great ones and bestow the vox. I am a guardian."

"Wait a sec." Colby tried to wrap his mind around what Keira was telling him. "You visit children at night after they lose their baby teeth. Are you telling me that...no...you're the tooth fairy?" Colby asked half joking, half serious.

"Tooth fairy!" Keira scowled. "That's a story made up by idiots to justify what they thought they saw. It's ridiculous." Colby didn't like her tone, but he did feel almost comforted by seeing her temper show, a trait that was definitely the old Keira.

She took a deep breath, calmed herself, and continued, "I suppose we are called tooth fairies in the English-speaking world. In the Spanish-speaking countries, they call us ratón de los dientes and that's a bit closer to our true nature. But, *we* call ourselves guardians. This was my first charge. You see, for each great one there's a guardian. The guardian calls her great one, her charge. That baby you saw, the one I was holding, he's my charge."

"Why was I there?"

"Sorry, my bad," Keira apologized. "Midnight is the magic hour, that's when it takes place, but I don't know what day I'll be called. It just happens at midnight after the tooth is lost. And since guardians don't know their charges, it's impossible to predict when that will be. I've been able to form the vox for months. I'm always at home by midnight in case I'm called, but tonight..."

The guilt that had been cloaked in confidence, now made its way to the surface. Keira stared at her hands clenched in fists, resting in her lap, "I was so wrapped up in my own stuff that I lost track of time and this night just happened to be the night. You were just sort of drawn in. Doesn't happen often, but it's not unheard of to have a stowaway."

"Stowaway" seemed like an odd choice of words, but Colby did not dwell on it. It was already too difficult to take in all this information. All the little things in his life that never quite added up, suddenly made sense. It was like someone had finally turned on the light. Keira's strange reaction in English class on the first day of school became clearer. In fact, this story cleared up a lot of questions that Colby had about his friend, except one.

"What's a mogdoc?"

"Where did you hear that word?" Keira was thrown. Colby could hear the sound of china hitting the floor in the kitchen. Obviously, his question shocked an eavesdropping Nana as well.

"Brooke said something about it," Colby replied.

"Well, I have to say, she's got more brains than I gave her credit for. I thought she bought that whole too much hairspray nonsense," she mumbled. "Mogdocs would be the evil. They try to prevent the great ones from receiving their gifts. Without the vox, the course of the charge's life would be very different."

"What do you mean?"

"Hmmm." Keira thought about that for a moment. "It would be kind of like trying to get through an underground tunnel without a flashlight. You may still find your way out, but it will take a lot longer and you might be too late."

"So basically, you light the path, protect the innocent, and save the world?"

Keira couldn't help but giggle. "Just call me Wonder Woman." Colby laughed for the first time since the event that opened his eyes and changed his life.

Nana returned to the living room with some cookies and milk. She listened intently as Colby helped Keira recount the tale of bestowing her very first vox. Gone was the anxiousness and rehearsed calm of their earlier conversation. Her excitement was now overwhelming and contagious. She told of how the "coil" pulled her to her charge, to the exact spot where she was needed. In a dramatic leap, she jumped on the coffee table to show the brilliance and the danger of the moment. She thanked Nana for training her so well, so that she could not only withstand the coil's effects but also handle the job at hand. She bragged about how flawless the whole event was, with the exception of a human stowaway of course. Although, Colby mentally noted that Keira mentioned pulling her dagger when she heard rustling that turned out to be a grunting Colby lying in the corner. He distinctly recalled no such weapon hidden in her sock. She didn't even have socks on. And there was something else...something that he didn't remember before. That one detail that Colby had seen through blurred eyes came rushing back.

"ACH," he muttered under his breath.

"What's that?"

"On the baby's blanket, I saw the initials ACH."

"Wow, now that I have his initials, maybe we can google him," Keira joked.

"No need," said Colby sternly. "I've seen that blanket before in my mom's hands...Andrew Christopher Hayes".

Chapter 10: Meet the Parents

The room fell silent. No one quite knew what to do with this new information. Was it just coincidence? Did it mean something?

Finally, Nana yawned and decided to turn in for at least a couple of hours before morning. Colby and Keira were still too wired to settle down. Keira finally had someone to confide in. Colby was someone whom she could trust to keep her secret. The two stayed up until dawn talking. They theorized about how Colby's nephew would save the world.

Soon daybreak peeked over the horizon and Colby decided to head home before he was missed. Keira swore him to secrecy one last time and gave him a hug. She had given him an old pair of rubber work boots and a jacket to wear home since he had been unexpectedly plucked from his bedroom wearing nothing but a t-shirt, sweats, and socks. He suspected that the boots and jacket were leftovers from Mr. Rickard, a kindly old man who checked in on the ladies once in a while to make modest household repairs. The boots were a bit small, the jacket a bit too big, and the walk home was extremely cold, but Colby didn't seem to notice. His life had gone from mediocre to marvelous in the course of one night. He just couldn't tell anyone about it.

He climbed into his window just in time to hear a knock outside the bedroom door. "Get up geek boy, Mom's got breakfast ready," an all-too cheery voice sang.

"School's out. Tell her I'm sleeping in," Colby shouted back as he kicked off his borrowed boots, chucked the jacket, and climbed under the covers of his inviting, warm bed.

He jumped up with a start. He recognized that voice. Just then, Jamie burst in the door.

"Hey! What are you doing here?" Colby asked.

"I was coming back from a business trip and decided to fly straight here." Jamie worked as a paralegal for a Cleveland company that did consulting and lobbying for major players in the food industry. He had only been in his job for six months, but was a fast learner and hard worker, so he quickly earned favor with the executive suite.

"I came in late last night to surprise Mom and Dad. Mary Sue's bringing Drew tonight." He rubbed his brother's head and gave him a playful punch in the stomach. "What's wrong? Didn't you get enough sleep last night?"

"Just go away," Colby grumbled pulling the covers back over his head.

"Okay, I guess I'll just go downstairs and let Mom know that you are sleeping in since you had a long night with Keira."

Colby growled from his nest of blankets. "What do you know and what do you want?"

"I know that little Miss Ryan climbed in your window last night. She's not the stealthiest intruder. Anyway, I heard you guys talking through the wall one minute and the next you were gone. Funny, I always figured that you were too chicken to climb down the trellis. Guess she's got you wrapped around her little finger. It was a shock, my perfect little brother sneaking out."

"What do you want?"

"Okay," he plopped down on the end of the bed. "Mom's got this idea in her head that she wants to take Mary Sue out for a 'Girls Day' tomorrow," he said complete with air quotes. "You know, she's thinking they'll spend a few hours at the salon, go shopping, and stuff like that."

"Yeah, so?"

"Mary Sue is freaking out. She's never left the baby for five minutes, let alone a whole day. Plus, she doesn't know Mom very well and she's super nervous about being alone with her all day. She doesn't want to hurt her feelings, but there's no way she's going. So, I was thinking that if you told Mom that you think everyone should spend Christmas Eve Day together, she'd go for it. After all, if perfect Colby thinks it's a good idea, how could she not agree."

"It's a deal. Now, let me sleep."

"Will do, ladies man" Jamie said and bopped out the door. "Nighty night, sleep tight," he sang in a high-pitched, girly voice.

Colby pulled the covers back over his head. The warmth of his big, soft comforter was fluffy relief. Christmas was just days away. A typical teenager, he had originally planned to avoid family time by staying in his room, but now he was looking forward to seeing his only nephew. Jamie, Mary Sue, and baby Andrew Christopher (Drew for short) would be staying in Jamie's old room which was right beside his bedroom. Drew would arrive tonight, December 23rd.

Colby drifted to sleep thinking these thoughts. His dreams were filled with images of little Drew in the Oval Office and little Drew leading an army into noble battle. Probably the funniest dream was of little Drew inventing cars fueled by dirty diapers. His dreams slowly moved from Drew to Keira. It would be her job to protect him and to see that he reached his full potential. Colby knew she was up to the challenge. He also knew that he would do whatever it took to help.

***

"What are you doing in bed?" Brooke barked.

"Huh...wha...," Colby rose startled. She pulled the comforter off his head. He noticed Jamie pass by the doorway in silence with a mischievous grin spread across his face. But, Brooke's attention was fully focused on Colby. She didn't even notice Jamie walk by.

"You were supposed to be ready. Lunch with my parents, remember? Oh, I can't believe you're not ready," Brooke said as she began pitching articles of clothing from Colby's closet. "Here, wear this," she said shoving a shirt and tie into Colby's half-awake face.

When he didn't respond, she stopped and looked at him suddenly realizing he was still very groggy. She noticed that his usually perfect hair was sticking straight up and his bewildered, innocent eyes stared at her. Her mood couldn't help but lighten at the sight of him. "Meet you downstairs in five minutes. And, Coco Bear, don't forget my present," she grinned and trailed out the door and down the stairs.

Colby rolled out of bed and into the pressed dress pants that Brooke had laid out. He had completely forgotten. This was the first time that he was to meet Brooke's parents. How could he forget? He had practiced making a good impression for two weeks. Of course, for the kind of kid that Colby was, first impressions were easy. He was studious, focused, and excelled at a wide vocabulary. He was good looking, polite, and always neat. If he was equally skilled at sports, he would be every parent's dream. Certainly, even Mr. and Mrs. Ethan Banes, III, would be impressed.

He wrapped a striped tie around his neck as he leapt down the stairs two at a time. His mother gave him a kiss on the cheek and handed him a small, tastefully gift-wrapped package as he darted out the door. He came upon the chauffeured town car, which was very similar to the limousine which Mr. Banes hired to take the gang to the Fall Ball. He entered and seated himself next to Brooke. Her mother was at

Brooke's other side and her father had taken the front passenger seat beside the driver.

Mrs. Alexa Banes was a tall, slender woman with voluminous, bleach blonde hair. On this day, her long nails were painted to match her fire-engine red dress suit. She wore black-trimmed glasses, which Colby suspected were fake, designed to make her appear more intelligent. She just had that way about her. She seemed to be someone of questionable intelligence, but impeccable taste.

Colby could tell little about Brooke's father. He could see that he had a full head of dark brown hair, professionally coiffed. He seemed to be of medium build and height. His nose was deeply buried in the business section of the daily newspaper; so much so, that he did not even acknowledge Colby's presence.

"I see you *have* decided to join us," Mrs. Banes sneered. Colby's hope for a brilliant first impression faded with the comment.

"I am so sorry. I had difficulty sleeping last night and…"

"No excuses young man. Tardiness speaks for itself."

The car fell silent. Colby felt that it was in his best interests not to pursue the point further, although he was surprised that Brooke did not intervene. She did flip through the items in her purse as if to draw attention away from Colby. Mr. Banes kept his nose buried in the newspaper.

"Is there any news about those missing kids from our school?" Colby asked in an event to make small talk.

Mr. Banes grunted.

They left their small town and drove into the neighboring city of Grant. The ride took only fifty minutes, yet it seemed like hours until they arrived at *Antonio's*. The driver hopped out and opened the door for the ladies. Colby took Brooke's arm, in an effort to impress her parents, and escorted her inside.

The owner, Antonio himself, came rushing to the podium as he saw them enter. "Hello, Mr. Banes, wonderful to see you," he said boisterously. "Your usual table?"

Mr. Banes simply nodded.

"I will seat you myself. Right this way."

He escorted them to a booth in a darkened corner of the restaurant. It was evident that this was a preferred table, as it was much more private than the other tables. Antonio handed them menus and brought a complementary bottle of red wine to the table. Colby noted that Antonio showed much respect, maybe even a little fear, for Mr. Banes.

Mr. Banes ordered for everyone in perfect Italian. It was the first words that Colby had heard him speak. He found himself staring at Brooke's father in amazement. Unfortunately, it didn't go unnoticed.

"What are you gaping at, boy?" Mrs. Banes snapped.

"I...uh..."

"Articulate too? Brooke, what are you thinking?"

"Mother, please."

"I spoke to your brother yesterday. He's doing so well. He finished his project and he's looking for his next one. Brooke, you should really talk to him. Perhaps he can help you meet someone."

Colby had never met Brooke's brother, but from what little Brooke spoke of him, he could tell that the guy was really driven and very stubborn. Brooke had said that he attended boarding school overseas. Mrs. Banes spent much of her time with her son; while, Mr. Banes seemed to spend more time with Brooke. Colby could tell that Brooke's mother had stepped over a line by mentioning her brother. Brooke's nostrils flared and she sat up straight, positioning herself to take the offensive.

"Mother, I assure you that Colby is special. I bet Father can see it."

Her dad had been reading emails on his phone since Antonio's departure from the table. He didn't even raise his head to answer, "Sure, princess."

"Father!"

He raised his head and took a deep breath. He stopped mid-inhale and his expression changed to one of interest. "Yes, I do think there is something special about this one."

Brooke seemed pleased with her father's confirmation. She smiled at Colby and took hold of his hand under the table.

Colby noticed that this interaction lightened the mood greatly. Now, Mr. Banes was present in both mind and body. He became an active participant in the conversation. This lessened the tension that Mrs. Banes seemed intent on creating. Mr. Banes asked him about all the right things: his academic achievements, his goals, and his family.

Just before dessert, Colby presented the neatly wrapped box to Brooke. She opened her Christmas gift with overwhelming excitement, ripping and tossing the paper aside. Of course it was instantaneously picked up by the restaurant staff. Within the wrapping was a black velvet box. She opened the box to reveal a white gold necklace. A solitary stone dangled from the chain. The stone was very unique, like two stones combined in one. The top of the stone was an emerald; the bottom sapphire. Colby explained, "This necklace represents us, love at first sight. We created something wonderful when my blue eyes met your beautiful emerald eyes. I hope you wear this and remember that I love you, Brooke."

Brooke hugged him tightly. Mr. Banes clapped his hands in approval. Mrs. Banes simply rolled her eyes in silent protest.

As they finished dessert, Mr. Banes was called away on business. He left the town car for them and asked Antonio to call him a taxi. Upon his departure, he shook Colby's hand and pulled him in. "This was certainly an interesting lunch. I am pleased that my princess has found you."

"Thank you, sir."

"And the gift, it was perfect. She is certainly very fond of all that glitters." He patted Colby on the back and smiled. "Curious cologne you're wearing. Is that what Brooke gave you for the holiday?"

"No, sir. I think Mom gave it to me for my birthday. I don't recall what it's called."

He sniffed a couple more times. "Yes, well," Mr. Banes said dismissively. "I hope that if you ever need help or advice, you will call on me. You can tell me anything, son." He passed Colby a business card and patted him on the back again as he left.

A few moments later, Colby, Brooke and Mrs. Banes set off for home. Once back in the town car, Mrs. Banes took the opportunity to shatter the confidence that Colby had worked up during lunch. By the time they pulled in front of his home, he was eager to leave the day behind. He quickly hugged Brooke goodbye, said a quick "nice to meet you" to Mrs. Banes, and ducked out of the car.

Chapter 11: Little Mr. Hayes

Colby burst into his house. He was so glad to finally be home. He kicked off his shoes, loosened his tie, and tried to shake the day's stress from his body. He plopped on the couch beside his dad and grabbed the remote control.

"Colby, is that you?" rang a voice from the kitchen.

"Yeah, Mom, I'm finally home."

"Come here, you have a visitor," his mom sang.

Colby's heart skipped a beat. He had been drug down from the strain of the day with Brooke's parents, but this lifted his spirits. He would finally meet Keira's charge, his nephew. He jumped to his feet, hopped over the back of the couch, and run into the kitchen. As he rounded the pantry, he did not see his brother Jamie or the baby. Instead, there stood Keira, licking the icing buttons from a gingerbread man.

"Glad to see me?" asked Keira with a broad smile. She knew very well that she was not the visitor he was expecting. Colby's shoulders fell. Without a word, he took a deep sigh and turned his back to her to open the fridge.

Lila always made a big to-do about Jamie's visits. Colby's dad, Curt, married young and was widowed before he even turned thirty. Jamie's mother died in a farming accident right after his first birthday, so the only mother he ever really knew was his step-mother, Lila. She never thought of Jamie as a stepchild, but cherished him as her own. Colby remembered times when Jamie would come home from college for just an overnight stay. Even then, she would meticulously clean every square inch of the house for a solid two weeks in advance. Of course, there was always a big family dinner involved and Colby's least favorite, home movies and scrapbooks.

"Keira has been a big help this afternoon. She helped me decorate all these Christmas cookies. Now everything's ready. And look Colby, she brought this adorable bib for the baby," Colby's mom said as she presented a shocking blue bib with the words "King of the World" imprinted on it.

Colby turned from the refrigerator, looked at the bib, then looked at Keira. She grinned mischievously and shrugged her shoulders.

"So let me get this straight. You let Keira help bake?"

"Of course not," his mother laughed. It was a well known fact that Keira was not the domestic type.

"I served as the icing design specialist and taste consultant on the project," Keira quipped.

Colby rolled his eyes and turned back to the refrigerator to grab a soda. As he moved to shut the refrigerator door, the doorbell rang. Colby slammed the door shut and took off running. Keira quickly followed. He strode through the living room and hopped over the coffee table as if it were a track hurdle. The short race briefly reminded him of the impromptu race to The Landing on that last day of summer. He felt Keira grabbing his shirt from behind to slow him down. However, Colby prevailed this time. He grabbed the brass latch and pulled open the large oak door. Mary Sue was standing outside. Little Mr. Hayes snuggled in her arms, bundled up tight.

"Come in. Come in," Colby shouted as he tried to catch his breath.

"What's wrong with you?" his older brother questioned. "I could hear you running to the door from all the way upstairs. You're not five anymore, geez, settle down." He pushed Colby aside and ushered his new family inside.

"Jerk, I'm just excited to see my nephew."

He reached for the baby and Mary Sue obliged. Colby sat on the bench in the entryway and worked to undo the puzzling myriad of snaps, straps, and belts on the baby's outerwear. By the time he had it all figured out, Colby's mother was standing over him, wanting desperately to hold her only grandchild. Colby passed Drew to her and everyone retired to the kitchen table to enjoy some Christmas cookies.

Colby could not help but stare at the baby. However, he noticed that everyone else seemed to have the same problem, though not for the same reason. He was a plump, alert thing with a few flyaway strands of platinum blond hair. His blue eyes darted around the room. Hard to believe that such a small, helpless child could one day change the world. Colby could see that Keira was captivated by the infant. He could also see that every time the baby caught Keira staring, he giggled and reached for her. Was she communicating with the baby in some unspoken way? Did the baby recognize her? Of course not, that is just silly, Colby thought to himself.

Then, Keira touched Colby's hand, looked him in the eyes and took a deep breath. No one noticed, except for Colby. It was time. As everyone else was busy chatting and making faces at the baby, she spoke up. "Can I hold him?"

Colby wondered if this was a monumental moment in guardian history. Had a guardian ever held their charge before…outside of the vox ritual? Had a guardian ever personally known their charge? He could see that Keira's eyes were tearing up, proof that this was indeed something special.

Lila handed the baby to Keira. "Remember to keep his head supported," she insisted, even though it was obvious that Drew was of age that he had no trouble lifting his head on his own.

Keira nodded and delicately took hold of the infant. He smelled of dried milk and baby lotion. His skin was soft and warm. When she smiled at him, he opened his mouth wide and giggled excitedly.

"Oh Jamie, he has his first tooth," Colby's mother boasted.

OF SUN & MOON

Colby asked Jamie, "When he gets older are you going to do the whole Tooth Fairy thing?"

His disguised taunt was not lost on Keira, who spoke up quickly. "Yes, I believe the plan is to have you visit in a pink tutu, wings, and a wand."

"That, I would pay to see," Jamie agreed.

"How much?" Colby laughed.

"Cut it out, boys" Lila insisted. With that, Drew let out a big yawn and rubbed his eyes.

"Keira, you are certainly a natural. Why, Drew's almost asleep. Go ahead and lay him down in the playpen that I've setup in the living room."

As she did this, she whispered, "I'll protect you with my life, kid."

Even though he was fast asleep, little Mr. Hayes let out a big, pleased sigh.

Chapter 12: Boys Night

By the 26th, Jamie was completely overtaken by cabin fever. This was the reason why he didn't come back to his small, rural home after college. When he was a teenager, he had often called it the most boring place on Earth. This feeling only intensified after moving away and experiencing life in the city. It seemed as though the whole town (except Walmart) shut down at six p.m.

Colby knew something was up when he overheard Jamie saying goodbye to Mary Sue.

"I promise. I won't be long. I've just got to do *something*," he said to her.

Mary Sue was very understanding. Not many women would be okay with being left alone in the middle of nowhere with her newborn and the in-laws that she barely knew.

Jamie turned and was headed down the stairs when he bumped into Colby.

"Where are you going?"

"Smitty just called. I'm headed to his place to watch boxing," Jamie said. "What's it to you?"

"Can I come too?"

"Why?"

"Hey, I want to get out of the house, just as much as you do."

Jamie thought for a moment. Colby knew that his older brother was taking his time in considering a worthy comeback. He was always a bit slower on the uptake than Colby. "What's wrong, didn't Kiki invite you to her tea party?" he finally managed.

Kiki…Colby hadn't heard that name in years. That's what Colby used to call Keira. The two had been friends since they could crawl and that was his first attempt at pronouncing her name. His Mom and Nana had thought it was adorable, so they encouraged it. He called her Kiki for the first five years of her life, only reverting to Keira when they started kindergarten, and then it was more of a Kei-wa.

"Come on man, I just wanna watch the fight," Colby pleaded.

Jamie grunted, then hesitated, then grunted some more, until he finally gave in. "Let's go, but I'm driving."

They hopped in Jamie's rental car and were soon at Smitty's doorstep. Colby had expected an apartment befitting a young bachelor, but was surprised to find that Smitty lived in a well kept, two-bedroom house on a quiet street. It was the kind of house that typically belonged to the kindly old lady on the block that baked pies for everyone. The house had white siding with red shutters and a big front porch with a swing. The outline of a Christmas tree took up the entire front window. Puffs of smoke were drifting from the chimney. The Smith house had that warm, homey feeling, complete with a huge evergreen wreath on the front door. It even had a white, picket fence.

Jamie knew it was the right place because the house used to belong to Smitty's grandmother before she passed away. Colby knew it was the right place because he could see Smitty's squad car parked outside the garage.

The two knocked on the door and he let them in right away. He was wearing a worn out rugby shirt and jeans that were ragged at the bottom. His hair was disheveled, like he had just woken up. He was barefoot and had a longneck beer in his hand. Colby was surprised to see this version of Smitty; the party guy he remembered, rather than the button-downed policeman he met the other day.

"Dude, my man, glad you could make it," he greeted Jamie. "And your little bro too. Listen, man, I am so sorry about picking you up the other day."

Jamie flashed an inquisitive look at Colby, but held back to listen.

"No problem. Any word on them yet?" Colby asked.

"We're looking into some alternatives, you know, trying to cover all the bases. When your name came up, I told the detective that there was no way that you were involved, but that guy won't listen to anybody. At the station, the rest of us think that if anyone's involved, it's that Edwards guy. My money's on him."

"Edwards?" Jamie asked.

"Yeah, the rich guy that used to have the big place on Front Street. You remember. He hired us to mow his lawn that one summer. "

"I know who you're talking about. That guy was loaded and didn't care what he spent. He paid us whether we mowed or not. That's the summer we were trying to raise money to go to Ft. Lauderdale. Man, what a trip."

"The Banes place?" Colby interrupted in an effort to keep the conversation on track.

"Yeah, and oh James, this Banes guy is the one that owns it now. Man, let me tell you, he's got a daughter that is a stone, cold fox. If I was sixteen again…"

Colby's face flushed. This didn't go unnoticed by the policeman who was used to being fully aware of his surroundings. "Oh, sorry, little bro. I totally forgot. She's your friend, right? She was with you when we picked you up."

"She's actually my girlfriend," Colby managed.

Smitty looked at Jamie, then to Colby with total shock.

"No doubt? That girl is smokin'," Smitty declared

"Yeah, she is."

They laughed all the way to the couch and plopped down in front of a full spread of junk food. Once everyone was comfortable, Colby delved back into the conversation, his true reason for the visit. "So, who's this Edwards guy that you mentioned?"

"Oh yeah, if you ask me, this Logan Edwards has 'perp' written all over him. He's wealthy, but no one knew where his money came from. He's a high level sponsor for the after school programs, so he has access to the kids. He has no family and no friends. Then, one day, he gets up, sells his house, and disappears. That sounds like someone who's up to no good to me."

"So how does he fit with Bobby and Shara?" Colby invited.

"My theory, and this is only between us, is that he's the one that kidnapped them and maybe even killed them. There are all kinds of possible motives. Maybe they were buying drugs from him and were going to turn him in. Maybe they witnessed a crime that he committed. Most likely, he was probably some weirdo that gets his kicks from taking kids. Anyway, he's gone without a trace. I think that someone found him out and took revenge. Maybe one of the parents got to him. The girl's parents left town. They said they had a commitment to Doctors Without Borders and couldn't get out of it. So, they're not even in the country now. It gets me thinking, you know? Logan Edwards is the perfect suspect; the question is, is he on the run or is he dead?"

By this point, Jamie was fully engrossed in the story and wanted more. "But if he is dead, where are they? I mean, the kids, where could they be?"

"That's the part that I can't figure out. Let's assume he's dead. Maybe he killed the kids and his murder was payback. Maybe a third victim killed him during escape and didn't know there were others. Maybe he nabbed them for someone else who killed him to insure his silence. Maybe he lied to his murderer about the kids' whereabouts and he died before they could find out where he really stashed them."

"Whoa. This town might not be as reserved as I thought," Jamie said. He tossed a piece of popcorn into the air and caught it in his mouth.

Chapter 13: New Year

Three days after Christmas, Jamie, Mary Sue, and little Drew headed home. Jamie had to go back to work because of the time off he had taken for Drew's birth. The Hayes house seemed empty and a bit sad. So, Colby was excited to get Jumper's call.

"Hey Hayes, got any plans for New Year's?" Jumper asked.

"Brooke's probably got something put together already, but I haven't heard yet. Somethin' going on?"

"Well, Ann and I thought it might be fun to do something as a group. Are you up for it?"

"What do you have in mind?"

"Rides at River Canyon then an all-night horror movie marathon at my house," Jumper said.

River Canyon was the local amusement park in Grant. Its rides weren't exactly multi-million dollar attractions, but the park's two coasters were killer and it was open until midnight on New Year's Eve.

"Sounds like a plan," said Colby. "I'll check with Brooke and call you back."

"Cool," said Jumper hesitantly.

Colby sensed there was more. "Something else?"

"Well, it's just…," Jumper stumbled over his words with uncertainty. "I…uh…Ann wanted me to call you…uh…she would have just called Brooke to clear everything, but…"

"What's up, Jump?"

"It's Ryan," Jumper finally spit out. "You know, she's not dating anyone right now, but she's still part of the group. Ann's all worked up about it. She probably won't be allowed to go anyway because of her strict curfew. Ann wanted me to ask you if we should invite her too or not? Will she be like a…" He chuckled, "…a fifth wheel?"

Colby hadn't thought of going without Keira. He just naturally assumed that she would be there. He imagined that Ann was struggling with this decision since Keira was one of her very best friends. He was sure that Ann was afraid that Keira would accept and then feel awkward about it, but also afraid that if she didn't invite her, Keira would be angry. Keira was known to hold a grudge. Colby always seemed to land in the mediator role. "I think she'd be cool."

"Good. If we need to set her up, I have a cousin."

"No way. Keira on a blind date? She'd kill you."

"You're right. Besides, I actually *like* my cousin. Anyway, don't clue her in on the fifth wheel thing. That line's just too good to waste; I'm totally using it that night," he joked. "You wanna call her?"

Colby agreed to call Keira after he talked to Brooke. He called Brooke directly and of course, she had already made plans. After some coaxing, she agreed to sell her tickets to the stodgy Midnight Gala and join in some teenage fun. Colby called Keira next. She was ready for some fun. Her midnight curfew was a thing of the past now that little Drew had received the first vox. "One charge at a time," she had told Colby. She wouldn't be called again until Drew was old enough to lose his first tooth and receive the second vox.

Once Colby completed his calls, he called Jumper back to confirm. "Great. See you then," Jumper said and hung up the phone. He was on the sofa in the family room with his girlfriend beside him.

"It's done. We're headed to River Canyon."

"And Keira's coming too?" Ann asked.

"Yep, just like you wanted."

The gang planned to meet at the front gates of River Canyon at nine. After the midnight fireworks, they would catch a ride from Jumper's dad back to his house, where they would spend the night. None of the parents had a problem with the co-ed sleepover. Jumper's dad was a respected and trusted church pastor in the community, so their parents knew that this small gathering would be well supervised.

Everyone arrived at the park well before nine. Colby was relieved to see that Keira did not back out. The group made their way quickly to the Screamin' Demon roller coaster and got in line. The cold winter night did not discourage the crowd of teens and college students in the park that evening. It was as busy as it would have been in the middle of July. Jumper and Ann stayed in the regular line, while Brooke and Colby moved into the front seat queue. Keira hung back until Jumper yelled "All fifth wheels in the back!"

Ann smacked Jump's arm and looked at Keira remorsefully. Keira really didn't care what Jumper said, but needed a break from him so she ducked between the bars and into the front line queue behind Colby and Brooke. She mostly stared at her boots in silence as the couple flirtatiously giggled and touched, completely ignoring her. As they moved forward in the line, the public displays of affection began to wane and Brooke's face grew whiter and whiter. Finally, she excused herself, grumbling something about the wind messing up her hair. However, it was evident that Brooke was too scared to ride. Keira didn't mind, this meant that she didn't have to ride alone.

Jumper and Ann boarded the train first. Ann waved goodbye to Colby and Keira who were still on the loading platform. Jumper made a sort of Dracula-esque maniacal laugh as the train clinked up the incline. "What a goof," thought Keira aloud.

Next it was their turn. Colby hopped in first, with Keira beside. He was a bit nervous, but he certainly was not going to let Keira see it. She sat as casually as if she were sitting on the sofa in her living room. "Okay, how do you want to pose for the camera on the last hill?" she asked.

"You're such a kid," Colby laughed nervously. He then blew the air out of his lungs and grasped the handles on his seat's vest, pulling it down over his head to fit securely across his chest. He clicked in the belt that linked the vest to the seat. The attendant walked by and gave each vest a quick tug.

This particular coaster had the traditional steep hill and valley leading into an impressive pitch-black tunnel which actually traveled underground, then up again, and into a series of cobra rolls before slowing into the station. It was a short ride, but definitely an exciting one.

The attendant pulled on the last vest and gave a thumbs-up signal to his co-worker in the control booth. The train gave a jerk then began to clink up the first steep incline. Colby closed his eyes, grasped his security vest tighter, and felt it pull up. They tipped over the top and Keira began to scream with delight. Her scream turned real as the safety belt that had been holding Colby's vest broke loose and flew past her. He leaned forward to grab the broken belt when his vest slammed up and struck his forehead. He sank motionless in the seat. Keira's vest then began to rise. She desperately held it down. For now, gravity was helping. Keira knew that soon they would be in the tunnel. Once they reached the dark tunnel, her chances of helping Colby before they hit the upside-down rolls would be slim.

Keira tried to keep her focus as the passengers in the seat directly behind them started screaming wildly. They had seen the faulty guards in the front seat and were frightened for their own safety.

Keeping one hand on the seat's safety vest, she moved the other hand to the inside of her jacket collar and pulled out her scarf. She took a deep breath before letting go. As she did the belt holding it down snapped and the vest flipped up into the air.

She worked quickly. She slid one end of the scarf around Colby's waist. She moved to his lap, pulling both ends of the scarf around them. She then drew his safety vest back down as closely as she could and laced the scarf through it. She made the final securing knot just as they entered the tunnel.

"Get off me! Where am I?" a groggy Colby asked.

"Hold on, Colby. We're still on the coaster. I've got us tied in."

Colby was shocked into full awareness. He wrapped an arm around Keira and grasped a side handrail with the other. She took comfort in this and closed her eyes momentarily. They would get through this, just one more minute and the ride would be over.

Then she opened her eyes to a flash of green piercing the darkness. "Mogdoc," she uttered breathlessly.

The green-eyed creature leapt from the wooden beams of the tunnel onto their coaster car. Keira could barely see the outline of its leathery skin, stretched taunt across its protruding bones like a bat's wings. It was small, but wickedly fast and vicious. It slashed the knotted scarf apart with its long, sharp claws. Then raised its arms and sucked in a deep breath allowing gills at the sides of its chest to flare. "For the glory of Bov, Edgund the Destroyer is victorious," the thing shrieked with a flick of its skinny, forked tongue.

"What's happening?" asked Colby from under Keira.

"Got it," Keira yelled back. She pulled her dagger from her right boot and thrust it into the creature's blue-gray skin. It screeched and swiped at

Keira's head. She pulled her head to one side to avoid the strike. This permitted Colby to see what was going on right in front of him. While Keira had it distracted, he grabbed the creature's skinny arm. It clamped its fangs on his wrist. Crying out in pain, he flung it onto the track ahead of them. They could hear its bones crunch as the coaster sped over it.

"We're loose," Keira shouted.

They burst out of the tunnel and were rising up the final hill before the cobra rolls that would take the coaster upside down. Keira was still in Colby's lap. She grabbed one end and Colby the other. They pulled the scarf back up around them, but it was now too short to tie off. She pulled at the vest, pleading for just a few inches more.

"I know," Colby said calmly. "Get back to your seat."

Keira slid over. Colby pulled her vest tight to her chest and secured it with the remaining bit of scarf.

"That's good. Now, how are we going to do this?" Keira asked.

The car had reached the top of the hill. Clink...clink.......clink.........

It teetered at the top, ready to drop at any moment.

"You have to be here to protect him," Colby said.

"No!" Keira screamed, pulling against her restraint.

Chapter 14: Questions

Everything went dark.

For a moment, Keira thought that she had blacked out. She then realized that the ride had shut down.

"Are you kids okay?" A hefty man wearing stained overalls and carrying a flashlight huffed up the metal maintenance catwalk affixed to the coaster.

Colby sighed with relief. He was alive. They both were. The other riders cheered. Keira pulled the scarf off her security vest and lifted it to free herself. She wrapped her arms around Colby and embraced him with all that she had. "Don't ever do that to me again," she whispered in his ear.

The passengers were assisted off the coaster one by one and led down the surprisingly stable, yet narrow, catwalk. Keira and Colby were the first off the ride. Ann, Brooke, and Jumper could not stand to wait at the exit. Worried for their friends, they moved to the bottom of the catwalk.

As soon as Colby reached the ground, Brooke pounced on him. "Coco Bear, I was so worried. What happened? Did Keira talk you into doing something stupid?" Keira lowered her head. She wasn't sure which bothered her more, that Brooke was blaming her or that Brooke was holding Colby.

"What? No," Colby replied. "It just broke."

"Both of them?" asked a man who appeared to be eavesdropping on their conversation. He stepped to Colby and held out his hand. "I'm Sal Sheppard, the night manager of this amusement park. I need to ask you a few questions. We'll also need to call your parents and I'll have someone take a look at that cut on your wrist. Please follow me."

"Cut?" Colby's mind was racing so hard that he didn't even remember the ripping bite of the mogdoc. Keira edged past Brooke, took the remaining bit of scarf and wrapped it around his wrist.

The next couple of hours in Sheppard's office were nearly unbearable. Colby and Keira separately recounted the ride in great detail. They spoke of how the safety vests broke apart on their own, even though they appeared to be intact at the start of the ride. Surprisingly, it was easy to leave out the part about killing a supernatural creature in the tunnel. After speaking with Nana and Colby's parents by phone and having the park medic bandage Colby's wrist, Mr. Sheppard issued each of them a lifetime pass to the park and released them to Pastor Johnson. Leaving the park, they passed the still darkened Screamin' Demon.

It would be closed for many months due to inspections.

The minivan was quiet on the way to Jumper's house. Pastor Johnson had made it clear that he was there to listen if anyone wanted to talk. However, no one wanted to. They were just glad it was over.

Still, Keira kept reliving the whole incident over and over in her head. Why would a mogdoc attack like that? She wasn't bestowing a vox. She wasn't even with her charge. She had never heard of such an incident before. Typically mogdocs only attack the charge; that's all they care about. They believe that guardians are worthless, human sympathizers. They wouldn't waste their time going after one, but this one did. And what was she going to do about Colby. He was going to die for her. Die! She had never before realized the peril that she put him in by sharing her secret. Keira was relieved to have the whole night to sort this out before talking to Nana.

When they arrived at the Johnson's everyone agreed that this was not the right time for horror movies, so Jumper thumbed through his video collection and pulled out *Christmas Vacation*. This seemed appropriate since Jumper and his father had not yet found time to pack away their Christmas decorations.

Keira immediately plopped down on the recliner nearest the T.V. Ann and Jumper covered the floor in front with pillows and blankets and spread out on their stomachs. Colby sat on the sofa behind them all. Brooke joined him. She snuggled close to him and he felt the same shiver that he did when they first met. He brushed her golden hair away from her face. She turned to look into his deep, blue eyes. "Do you know that you're perfect?" she asked stroking his bandaged wrist.

"Oh, brother," Keira mumbled, but they didn't hear.

As always, the coolness of Brooke's breath against his skin intoxicated him. "Just because I'm with you," Colby said.

"I just don't know what I would have done if..."

"Shhh." In that instance, he could not think of anywhere else he'd rather be. He took her face in his hands and their lips met softly. Then Brooke nestled her head on his shoulder and drifted to sleep in his arms.

She had pretended not to hear. In fact, she had pretended to fall asleep. However, a single tear escaped down Keira's cheek as she fought to keep her breathing soft and even. She prayed that sleep would take her quickly.

Chapter 15: Edgund the Destroyer

By morning, Colby definitely wanted to talk to Keira. He wanted to see what was going on; what he could do to help. But, Keira slipped out as soon as the sun peeked over the horizon. She had a lot to discuss with Nana.

Nana was in her fluffy light blue bathrobe and slippers when Keira poked her head in the kitchen door. She was calmly sipping her morning tea.

"Oh my dear, sweet girl," she said softly. She rose to embrace Keira and kissed her gently on the top of her head. "Can I get you something to eat?" she asked as she fussed about the kitchen and started to pull out an iron skillet from the drawer beneath the oven.

"No, I'm not hungry," Keira said flatly. "It wasn't an accident."

"What do you mean?"

"It was a mogdoc."

"Are you certain?"

"Yeah. I didn't see it at first, but in the dark, it made itself known. I stabbed it with my...oh no."

"Dagger...You left your dagger behind?" Nana finished her sentence.

"Yes, stuck it in the thing. Colby tossed it off of us, he wouldn't have even thought about the dagger. You should have seen us in action."

"My Colby?" Nana asked. It wasn't surprising. Colby and Keira were such good friends, that Keira's house had become a second home to him. Nana had grown to think of him as one of her own.

"Yes, your little Colby."

Nana didn't smile, but instead, shook her head in disbelief. "Where was the baby?"

"That's just it, Nana. My charge wasn't even there. Jamie headed back to Cleveland earlier this week. It was just Colby and me. From what I could tell, our seats had the only safety harnesses that it sabotaged," Keira explained. "It was definitely one of Bov's. It yelped something about Bov's glory, and it had a nefarious name, called itself the...what was it....the punisher...no, the destroyer."

Nana's face turned white. Her teacup dipped slightly, but she caught it before even a drop spilled. "Think carefully, dear. Was that, Edgund the Destroyer?"

"Yeah, Edgund, scary name, huh?" Keira laughed. Then, she noticed that Nana wasn't laughing.

"You're saying that you believe Bov Gammen sent Edgund the Destroyer after you."

"Yeah, I think so. Everything's all right, I killed this thing. It's definitely dead. The coaster squished its guts out."

"Come with me," Nana ordered. Her tone had changed from sweet and concerned to focused and cold.

Keira followed her up the stairs to Nana's bedroom. Nana pulled back the chair at the delicate, antique vanity positioned in the back of the room. Keira reflected on how, when she was a little girl, she admired the beautiful, hand-carved scroll work on this piece of furniture. She recalled that she couldn't understand why the vanity stood in the darkest corner of the room, instead of by the window. Of course, that was before she knew its true purpose.

"Mirror, Mirror, on the wall," Keira said flippantly.

Nana gave her a reprimanding look and pushed the vanity mirror back into the wall. The mirror glowed with a brilliant white light and expanded to the size of a door. Nana and Keira stepped through it, into the training room.

Once they were inside, the mirror shrunk to its normal size behind them. The guardian training room looked very much like an old, grand library. The ceiling was a dome of glass framing the starry sky. Even if it was daytime or overcast outside the rest of the house, it was always midnight under a clear, full moon sky in the training room. Besides the moon, the only light came from a few, lit candles scattered across the room.

It was a round room, two stories high. The second floor was open to the first with full bookcases and a couple of small desks lining the walls. An iron railing forged to look like a tree's entwined branches overlooked the first floor, which was mostly open for physical training. The north wall held open shelves where a vast arsenal of antique and modern weapons and training tools such as pads and dummies were stored. The east side held a clear glass case, about the size of a telephone booth. It was the most extraordinary of all the objects in the room for inside was a red swirling wind, a captive coil.

Without hesitation, Nana climbed the spiral stairs and headed straight to the third bookcase. Keira followed closely behind and plopped down at the first desk. "Here it is," Nana announced as she pulled an ancient-looking, leather-bound book from the shelf and moved to Keira's desk. The book was a much worn, brown leather tome. She retrieved her glasses from her robe pocket.

Nana flipped through the ancient pages quickly. Keira looked over her shoulder, scanning the text for something familiar. "Edgund the Destroyer," she read.

She pointed the lines out to Nana who continued to read the selection aloud. "Mogdoc...loyal noble of the empire...master saboteur...skilled assassin...decorated member of the Sect of Low."

Keira gulped. She pulled away from the book as if it were a snake that was about to strike. "Sect of Low," she whispered under her breath. Shaking her head, she crossed her arms at her chest. "I remember them, but they're just legend. Weren't they Gammen's best warriors, sort of his own version of the knights of the round table?"

"Something like that," Nana said as she removed her eyeglasses and slipped them back into her robe. "The mogdoc royal guard, they are the worst of the worst and they stop at nothing. It was believed that there were six members of the Sect of Low."

"Guess that's down to five."

"Unless they've recruited more…" added Nana thoughtfully. "Of course, we have to be prepared."

"I still don't understand why it was here…now. The charge is vulnerable only during the vox exchange between guardian and charge, that's Mogdoc 101. Why didn't it try then? Why did it go after me instead? Why send a member of the Sect? Why did it crawl out of its muddy cave to bother with Colby?" Keira was full of questions. "Muddy cave?"

"Oh," she gushed as a new revelation hit her. Her knees buckled. "They found muddy footprints when Bobby and Shara were taken. What if the Sect is behind the abductions?"

Nana considered this for a moment, and then slowly spoke. "I'm afraid we don't have all the information we need," she replied. "You've had a long night. I'll fix you some breakfast, go wash up."

Nana gave her a hug before leaving the training room. It was meant to be comforting, but it just wasn't enough. After Keira had gone to splash some water on her face, Nana set the book down with a sigh. She composed herself and leaned over a candle situated on the desk. She moved so closely that her lips nearly touched the flame. She whispered into it, "Tell them the prophecy is coming to pass."

The flame turned pale blue with her words. It rose up in a small ball of light with a long tail behind. The glowing ball swept past Nana's head with great speed. It swirled up to the top, centermost point of the room and disappeared.

Chapter 16: What's in a Name

Colby finally caught up with Keira at school on Monday. She was at her locker searching for a stick of gum, when he approached. "We've got to talk," he said and she agreed to meet him in their secret room behind the chem lab during third period. Colby waited behind the sunflower and rainbow door for the entire fifty minutes. There was no sign of Keira. At lunch, he scanned the commons and still no Keira.

Ann told him not to worry. "She probably just wants to be alone. That was a close call you two had on New Year's and she's not the kind to keep feelings locked up. I'm sure she's just blowing off some steam," she said in a failed effort to soothe him.

"Tell ya what, if she's not outside at the fountain after school, I'll help you look for her,"

Jumper offered. This made Colby feel better. Inside, he knew that they were probably right. In all likelihood, Keira would be at the fountain to walk home with him. She could tempt fate by skipping school, but she would never unnecessarily risk being caught by Nana.

Sure enough, when the last bell rang, Colby found Keira walking the edge of the fountain as if it were a tightrope. He walked past her without stopping. She jumped off the ledge and jogged a few steps to catch up with him. She walked silently beside him.

They walked and walked and walked and were almost home before Colby broke the silence.

"So where have you been all day?" He kept his gaze straight ahead, fearing that he would back down if he had to look her in the eyes.

"Just here and there."

"Are you ready to talk now?"

"Sure. What do you want to know?"

He stopped. He stared at her in disbelief. "Just start at the beginning," he finally said. "What *really* happened on New Year's Eve?"

Keira looked from side to side to make sure that no other human was within earshot. She spoke quietly and calmly.

"That thing on the roller coaster was a mogdoc. Actually he is, I mean was, sort of an infamous mogdoc. Nana says that he was one of Gammen's best assassins."

"Gammen?"

Keira stopped in her tracks. She was finding it very hard to remember what Colby did and did not know about her world. She had opened the floodgates by sharing her secret. Now, she was finding it hard to stop. She would need to explain. "Bov Gammen is the leader, well, technically emperor, of the mogdocs. He's the third Gammen to rule and I know it's hard to believe but he's supposed to be even more ruthless than his father."

"His father?"

"Bo Gammen," she offered. He shook his head.

"Gimme a break, Colby, Bo Gammen, was so feared, so evil, that his name was spread across the entire world in warning, never to be forgotten. Ring a bell?"

"I'm telling you. I've never heard of him before."

"Yes, you have," Keira insisted.

By this time, they had arrived at her front door. He followed her inside. They made their way quickly through the tiny living room and into the kitchen which overlooked the back yard. "We're home, Nana," Keira yelled over her shoulder. Colby took a chair at the kitchen table as Keira pulled a couple of orange sodas from the fridge.

Keira continued her story, "I guarantee that you've heard of Bo Gammen. You probably just don't realize it. Let me just jog your memory a little. You know, mogdocs live for hundreds of years."

"Sure, I think I learned that in mogdoc biology class."

"Whatever, point is, we're talking about an ancient evil, before there was internet, television or even, radio. His name was passed by word of mouth, even across the barrier. By the time mutterings of his name reached the Americas, it got a little twisted and the pronunciation changed a bit. You're smart. Think about it and say his name a few times quickly."

Colby said it in his head at first. Still searching for the answer, he spoke it aloud, "Bo Gammen... Bo Gammen... Bogammen..... Boogammen...... Boogeyman."

Colby was speechless. Keira nodded. "When his name spread, he was weakened. That's how it goes with the older creatures, their power comes from their true name. Mortals fear the unknown evil; but once it's named, it loses potency. As his true name spread, he eventually had to step down and his son, Bov, assumed the throne."

"What? That can't be right," Colby rationalized. "Next you're going to tell me that werewolves and vampires really do exist."

Keira shrugged but didn't answer.

After a few minutes of silent thought, Colby decided the best approach would be to get back to the issue at hand. "Do you think that he'll send another assassin?"

The last trace of a smile disappeared from her face. "No."

"Good."

"I think he'll try to finish the job himself."

She closed her eyes. She could feel Colby's hand move to her shoulder. "You'll be okay. I'll do whatever you need me to do."

She kept her eyes shut and could feel his closeness. Her heart began to pound. She wanted to be selfish. She wanted to keep him by her side, even if it put him in danger. She had never wanted anything more. She lifted her hand to his cheek and he moved away, oblivious to the moment.

"I've not been afraid of the boogeyman since I was seven and I'm not gonna start now. And at least you'll see him coming. It's not like he can just waltz into school and..."

"Actually, he can. The Gammens are powerful shapeshifters. That's why they've ruled for so long. His true form is mogdoc, but he could appear to be anyone he chooses. It's also rumored that Bov has a special power over humans. Supposedly it's like mind control, but over just emotions, not actions."

"You mean he could tell the lunch lady to dose your cafeteria food with poison?"

"Not exactly. It's not actions, just emotions. He couldn't order her to do it, but he could make her feel extreme loyalty or love, then, ask her to do it as a favor. She may not be able to resist."

"Whoa."

"I know. Now, if you'll excuse me, I've got to pack my lunch for tomorrow."

Chapter 17: Be Mine

It was Valentine's Day and the school was bursting with love sick teenagers. Gestures of affection were in abundance, culminating with Jumper serenading Ann with his own rendition of "Love Me Tender" in the crowded commons during lunch. He had solicited help from the glee club which outfitted him with background music, a microphone, and even a sequined jumpsuit.

Amid the commotion, Keira did get a chance to sneak in a quick "Happy Birthday", which meant a lot to Ann. She hated that her birthday was one of those holiday birthdays that everyone tends to forget. It was nice to know that her best friend remembered.

This made Keira feel good about herself too, at least for a little while. However, the feeling was fleeting. The stress of her current situation with Emperor Gammen combined with a day full of sugary sweet mush was, by far, more than she could take. Finally, the end of the school day came and she was eager to see Colby and head home. She could always depend on him, her best friend, her Colby. Unfortunately, she arrived at the fountain outside, just in time to find him locked in a tight embrace with Brooke.

"Ugghh! Not you too," she muttered.

Colby didn't hear her. He was so thoroughly wrapped up in his girlfriend's eyes. However, Brooke did hear.

"I wish you could stay here with me a little longer, but you had better take little Keira home," Brooke sneered.

Colby looked to see a disgruntled Keira standing ten feet away from them. "Oh, she can wait. You want me to stay."

"If only we could, but my Dad's waiting for me. I'll text you later," she said as she kissed his cheek and broke his embrace. His eyes followed her as she strutted to the street and slid into the back seat of the parked town car. He continued watching as it zoomed away from the curb.

"Wow," he muttered. He stepped dreamily to Keira. "She's....wow."

"Oh, please."

And with that Keira bounded down the path toward home. She took the lead, staying two paces or more ahead of Colby, cursing under her breath most of the way.

As they approached the last bend before Keira's house, Colby's mind finally cleared of Brooke.

He then noticed Keira's impatience with him and became annoyed. He yelled to her, "Are you too good to walk beside me now?"

"Fine," she said stopping in her tracks. She turned to him and crossed her arms at her chest almost as if she were trying to hold herself back. "Here's the deal."

She shifted her weight to her left leg, then back again to her right. Colby could almost see the internal struggle that was raging inside Keira. He took her hands in his. Nervously, she squeezed them tightly. It was too tightly. She really didn't know her own strength.

Yet, he didn't pull away. She gritted her teeth and looked over his head. She could feel her emotions trying to burst out. She had held them back for far too long. "I just can't ignore this anymore. I can't stand to see you with her. You're not supposed to be with her. I think I love you, Colby. That's all."

"What do you mean?"

Keira couldn't help but think that even for a boy, he was being completely dense. She felt her eyes begin to tear as she looked into his. "You almost died for me. You're supposed to be with me."

"Is that what this is all about?"

"That's what it's been about. That's all I can think about; not Gammen, not the Sect, just you and what you were willing to do."

"Keira, listen to me. You're not in love with me. Not really."

"You're the only one I trust completely. When I'm not with you, I feel almost broken and all I can think about is the next time that I'll see you," Keira said in one continuous breath.

Colby dropped her hands and shook his head.
"I just...I just want you to hold me, like you
hold her. I want to feel safe."
He opened his mouth, but no words came out.
"Say something. Please," Keira begged.

***

A few miles from Keira and Colby, the very
same words were being spoken by another.
"Say something. Please," Ann's father begged.
"It's a lot for her to take, Bob," Ann's mother
encouraged.
"I think it's super awesome," her little sister,
Katie, cheered.
Ann just rolled her eyes at the three of them. It
was *her* birthday after all. She was expecting cake and
maybe a new phone or clothes, but not this.
Her father adjusted his glasses nervously. He
couldn't fathom why she hesitated to take her place in
their family. "Ann, I need your formal answer. This is
your birthright. As the eldest in your generation, it is
up to you to accept or decline."
"My birthright! My birthright? You've only
just told me about this and I'm supposed to make my
decision right now."
His eyes softened and her mother, who had
been watching the whole scene, decided to step
forward. She placed a hand on Ann's shoulder. It
steadied and comforted her. When she started to speak,
her voice was soothing.
"Ann, this isn't a gift. This is what we are. As
the eldest, if you deny it, you deny it for your
generation of the family, including Katie. Plus, if one

day you have children and they accept their heritage, you will not have the experience to guide them to use it wisely."

Katie plopped down on the couch and began pouting, sure that her practical sister would pass on this incredibly cool birthday surprise.

Her mother continued, "You worry too much, Ann. We trust you. You are smart and responsible. You can handle this. In fact, you will be one of the most respected travelers in the history of our kind."

"You're just saying that because you're my Mom."

"I'm saying it because it's true," her mother smiled. "And you will guide your sister to be the same. Together you can do anything. Accept this. You deserve it."

"Please Annie, this is so cool," Katie badgered.

Ann nodded. Her mother always knew exactly what to say to make her feel better, but then her Dad chimed in.

"Before you decide, there's one more thing we have to tell you. If you decide to accept and use your ability, it will be up to you to help your mother and I keep a promise."

He really did have bad timing.

***

Elsewhere, Keira was becoming increasingly impatient with her other best friend.

"I don't know."

Keira let out a long breath. She could feel her heart fall to her stomach. "Just forget it."

"Don't be upset. I just...I need a minute," Colby explained. He followed and was soon beside her again. "Why now?"

Keira could feel her temper rise. Did he think this was just a whim, a crush, a jealous reaction? Maybe it was. She counted to ten slowly in her head and tried to give him the benefit of the doubt as she spoke. "Colby, I understand that you don't feel the same, so forget it. Let's just drop it."

"I can't."

"Keira? Keira!" Nana yelled from the front porch.

They looked up to see two strangers standing with Nana. She was standing between them with her arms around both of their waists, almost as if she were presenting them. The man to Nana's left was tall and looked to be in his early thirties. Even under his navy sweater and khakis, he seemed to be very slim and muscular. He was ruggedly handsome with slightly tousled black hair and a bit of a five o'clock shadow. The woman to Nana's right was just as beautiful as the other stranger was handsome. Her long, shiny black hair was perfectly straight and trimmed to just below her collarbone. She looked to be roughly the same age as the man. Her long legs were clad in black dress pants and smartly topped with a red sweater set and delicate pearl necklace. The strangers' huge, white smiles were distracting.

"Keira, there are two people here who would like to speak with you," Nana rang. "Goodbye Colby".

"Whatever they want to say to me, they can say in front of Colby."

"Colby, why don't you go on home? I'm sure that Keira will call you later."

"Keira, maybe I should..." Colby tried to reason, but was cut off by Keira and her mounting temper.

"No, he's staying."

Now embarrassed, Nana dropped her arms from the couple and moved toward Keira. Her smile was fading. "Keira, I don't think you understand," she said through her teeth now gritted to sustain her grin.

When Nana got close enough, Keira whispered, "Do you know these people? Why are you letting strangers in our home at a time like this?"

"Let's let them explain." She nodded toward Colby. "Good night, I assure you that everything is fine. I'm sure that Keira will call you later to tell you all about it."

Colby looked to Keira. She nodded. So, he said a quick good night to Nana and continued down the path toward home. Nana wrapped her hands around Keira's arm and dragged her to the porch. "Come on, kiddo, you're finally going to get what you've always wanted."

Nana placed Keira directly in front of the couple for their inspection. "She's lovely," the woman gasped. She pulled her clasped hands to her mouth in awe. Now that she was close, Keira could see that the beautiful woman had been crying. Her eyes were still red and wet with tears.

"She doesn't even know who you are," the man commented. He smirked and relaxed his stance, placing his hands in his pockets. "You're probably creeping her out, Bianca".

Keira knew that name. A wave of recognition crossed her face. "Mom? Dad?"

The woman stepped forward and embraced her so quickly that Keira did not even see her move. The man's nonchalant expression broke and his eyes started to tear. "What you must think of us," Bianca cried. "We have so much to talk about."

Nana ushered the reunited family inside. Her own eyes now tearing, she wiped them dry with a fresh tissue from her skirt pocket. The couple quickly sat down on the sofa. Nana pulled up a chair beside them. Keira was still in shock and could not move from the doorway. She would not take her eyes off them.

"Please, sit with us. It's been so long, too long" said the man that Keira now recognized as August Ryan or more appropriately, Dad.

He patted the space between his position and his wife. Keira cautiously moved to them and sat slowly between them. "Why are you here?"

Really, she wanted to ask, why are you so nice or why are you acting like you like me? She'd always dreamed of facing her parents, of telling them off for being so selfish. *That* was her reality, not this.

Bianca started to sob. August reached behind Keira to stroke Bianca's back in a soothing way. Nana interrupted, "Perhaps this discussion will be easier in the training room."

"Of course, the library," Bianca lifted her head.

The family moved down the hallway. Nana first, then Bianca and August, with Keira following. August lightened as he recognized the antique vanity in the darkened corner of Nana's bedroom. He pushed the vanity mirror. It glowed with a brilliant white light. They paused and Bianca fidgeted with her sleeves. She took a deep breath and they entered the training room. Once all four were inside, they moved toward the first set of bookcases.

Nana pulled out a step ladder and balanced on her tiptoes. From the top shelf, she pulled a book bound with a heavy red cover. The pages were edged in gold. As she pulled it from the shelf, she opened it to a bookmarked page and glided to the desk.

"Keira, this is why we had to protect you," Bianca said.

Keira lost it. This was just the last straw. "Protect me. How dare you. I've never met you, now you show up out of the blue and say you've been protecting me…because of a book."

"Keira!" Nana warned.

"No, she has every right to be upset with us." Bianca looked desperately to August for help.

"Keira, you are very special, we've always known that you are more than a guardian and now we believe that Bov knows it too."

"We never wanted to leave you. It was agony…" Bianca choked on her tears. "But we had to, to save you. He would have known that you existed and he would have…" her sobs completely took over.

Keira's throat tightened and she struggled to gulp a new breath. Her knees buckled, but August caught her before she hit the floor. Why did they send Colby away? She knew that she needed her solid friend now. This was more than she could bear.

"This is what started it all, Keira," August said pointing to a page in the book. "It's a prophecy that has been handed down through many, many generations of guardians. It was written by a charge blessed with prophetic sight."

Keira stared at the words on the page. She struggled to see them clearly through her tear-drenched eyes. It read:

> *A child born of sun and moon will*
> *impart a human gift to bring forth*
> *the fall of the house of Gammen.*

"Of sun and moon," Keira read aloud. August's eyes darted to Bianca, who again dropped her head sobbing.

"We believe this prophecy is about you, Keira," August said. "I am the moon, your mother is the sun."

"Right." Keira clamped her hands over her head. "This is ridiculous."

August's eyes darted back to Bianca. She wiped away her tears and lifted her head. She looked lovingly into August's eyes then turned to Keira and brushed her hair from her face. "Your father is like the moon. He is a protector, just as the moon watches over the earth." She sniffed and continued, "I'm like the sun, not a protector, not a guardian".

"But of great benefit to the world," August resumed and took Bianca's hand.

It clicked. "A charge...*His* charge," Keira suddenly understood. She grabbed her mother's wrist and turned it to see a smashed copper coin dangling from a tiny bracelet. It had rough edges and was engraved with swirls and strange symbols circling the universal figure eight symbol for eternity.

"I knew it," Keira burst. "No humans in the training room, but you have an Atlantis token."

"Yes," the two confirmed. Bianca pulled her sleeve back down nervously to cover up the trinket. August moved on to clarify. "You know that on this side of the barrier, time moves much, much slower. That's where I lived, but I was young and curious. I wondered what became of my first charge. So, I crossed the barrier to seek her, to see the future that she made possible. When I returned, instead of a child, I found a beautiful, smart, young woman…my other half. She had grown to become my perfect Bianca and it was love at first sight. We were married in secret."

Bianca picked up the story, "We were happy, making a life for ourselves among humans. We even started a family. Your father knew the prophecy. He knew that Gammen took it seriously. So, we took every precaution to make sure that no one would know that God and our love created a child. At least, that's what we believed. But he came," she stared into August's eyes trying to find the strength to finish. "He was one of Gammen's minions. An untalented fortuneteller, whose visions were more often wrong than right. He decided to check out his vision first hand before alerting the emperor."

"To Bov, incompetence is punishable by death," August explained.

"That is what saved you. August was able to destroy the mogdoc quickly. Still, we couldn't be sure that there wouldn't be others to follow, so we had to….sever…our connection."

Bianca dropped her head again in uncontrollable sobs. Like partners in a tag team match, August tagged back into the story, "We made it safe for you here; then we distanced ourselves by crossing the barrier and living on the other side. No one but Nana and your protectors would know that we ever had a child that could threaten Gammen's reign."

Keira's body relaxed. Finally! Something she could wrap her head around. There was so much that she couldn't. "You sent me away because you thought Gammen would try to kill me to stop the prophecy?"

"Yes, we sent you to hide and train with a wise, and powerful, old friend." Keira turned to see August staring directly at Nana.

"Yeah," Keira nodded. "She's trained me well. My first vox went smoothly. But..."

"Your first vox!" August exclaimed. His formal attitude disintegrated and all that was left was pure giddiness. He was like a father, seeing his baby walk for the first time. He jumped up and clinched Keira's shoulders. "I can't believe it! My little girl, all grown up."

"Okay, Dad."

It was odd to use that word...Dad. She couldn't help but notice how clumsily it dropped from her mouth. She hoped that the awkwardness was not apparent to him. Well, that's not entirely true. She hoped that it caused him a little bit of guilt. Perhaps if she tried it again, "Dad, I just don't think I'm ready to face Gammen. I don't know anything about this human gift and I think Gammen took these two kids from school."

"It's okay," he assured her. "The traveler was watching over the party. He was able to get that girl off the street just after the party. Her family took her out of the country to a safe place. They'll sort it out with the authorities when this is all over."

"What about Bobby?"

"Unfortunately, we didn't know about the boy until after he'd been taken. As for the prophecy, your human gift, it will become clear in time."

"I'm so tired of waiting."

Nana cleared her throat. "If I may interrupt, I sent you the message because I think the time is now."

Bianca asked, "What do you mean?"

"The Sect is after your daughter and there's this…" Nana closed the book. For the first time, Keira could see the cover. It was a luxurious, brilliant red with the title printed in golden script, *The Hayes Prophecies*.

Bianca and August stared at Nana for the answer that Keira could see right before them.

"I thought it was a coincidence. You and Colby are just friends. It's not an uncommon last name," Nana rushed to explain. Keira looked to her parents and momentarily relished the fact that she was not the one in the dark this time. Nana continued, "Now that we know your charge shares the same name, the same family, I have to think that it's more than that."

This was enough information for August to grasp a conclusion. "You believe that your charge is a descendent of Cohen Hayes, the author of the prophecies," he stated for everyone's benefit. "Amazing."

"So what do I need to do?" asked Keira.

August considered her question carefully. "Lay low. We're not sure what this means. Go about your normal business. We can protect you in the meantime. The baby should be protected since mogdocs can't sense charges, except at the exact hour when the vox is bestowed. That's the only vulnerable time. It will be a few years before you're called again. The second vox will be given when he loses his first tooth."

Nana asked, "What about Colby?"

"Is that the cute boy you were with this afternoon?" Bianca chimed.

"Yes, the *Hayes* boy," Nana emphasized.

"Wait, I'm confused again," Bianca said. "He's too old for the first vox."

"Two of them! Amazing," August exclaimed. His eyes were opened wide and nearly all of his pearly white teeth were showing in his giddy smile. "I can't help but think that our little darling is a bit of an over-achiever, Bianca. The prophecy asks her for one human and she's already got two lined up."

"Stop that," Bianca said as she playfully pushed August. "You're embarrassing her."

"Okay, you're being weird."

They silenced and settled into preparation mode. Keira retreated to a comfortable reading chair in the far corner of the training room as Nana and her parents began making defensive plans. Even from across the room, she couldn't take her eyes off them. She reflected on the affectionate playfulness of her parents and could see why August chose the words, "my other half". They seemed to truly be two halves of one, from their tag team storytelling to their constant, loving gaze on each other.

Bianca strolled over to Keira and stood behind her. She leaned over and took Keira's hair in her hands, stroking it gently, and pulling it back from her face. It felt good. "Mom?" Keira noted the peculiarity of saying the word aloud.

"Yes, sweetheart?" Her voice was shaking. She was teetering at the brink of yet another round of sobs.

"I have to know. You're a charge, a great one, so…" The words were harder than she thought they would be, but Keira continued. "Were you able to change the world before you met Dad? Or did you two alter the master plan by falling in love?"

Of course, what she really wanted to ask was if her birth destroyed her mother's destiny.

Bianca laughed gently. "Can't you see how I've made this world better? Yes, Keira, I was able to make my contribution to change the world," she said. "You are the contribution that I'm honored to have brought to the world. You are meant for great things, Keira. You will save the world."

Keira smiled and felt peace. She quickly drifted to sleep in her mother's safe arms.

Chapter 18: Campfire Story

In the weeks to follow, things returned to normal. Well, at least as close to normal as they could be. August and Bianca stayed at Nana's. Their days were full of preparations and planning; while their nights were reserved for leafing through old photo albums, listening to Nana's stories, and catching up on their daughter's life.

Keira told Colby about her newly reunited family. Her parents thought that it would be best to keep the prophecies a secret; so she simply told him that they gave her up to protect her anonymity as a guardian. That satisfied his interest. His friend's new outlook on her family pleased him. The discussion they had on the afternoon of her parents' first visit was unresolved, but Colby still had Brooke in his life and

Keira had the love of her parents. That was enough for now.

The cold winter wind changed to the unrelenting showers of spring which then, transformed into the warm breezes of early summer. Jumper decided it was time for a camping trip to celebrate the end of the school year.

For Jumper, it was an annual rite of passage. He loved nature and sleeping under the stars rejuvenated him for summer. He always looked forward to it. His Dad, Pastor Johnson, called it the Survival Revival, touting it as a way to commune with God and witness the full power of his creation. The Teen Leaders group from the good pastor's congregation was going. Jumper also invited Colby who was definitely more comfortable inside, but reluctantly agreed to join them.

This year's destination was the woods of northern West Virginia. Fishing and hiking were at the top of everyone's agenda. The group pitched a handful of tents, which were mostly unused.

"Real men don't need tents," Jumper challenged. Colby didn't care. He was already giving up electricity and modern plumbing. He was not going to give up his nylon sanctuary.

On the second evening, Colby ducked into his tent to grab a jacket before dinner. They had done well at the river that day; five bass, four big catfish, and a dozen bluegill. Pastor Johnson was showing the boys how to prep the fish for cooking, when Ann hiked into camp.

Jumper's face lit up like the Christmas tree at Rockefeller Center. He ran to her, picked her up and twirled her around. "I guess my surprise is a hit," she smiled.

The other guys were delighted to see her too. Well, maybe not so much her, but her four dozen triple chocolate brownies were certainly appreciated. She even had a special gift for Colby, from Keira.

"It's a 100-watt bulb for my battery-operated lantern. This is very thoughtful, I guess?" Colby managed.

After dinner, they settled around the campfire for ghost stories. Jumper told the old one about the killer with a hook for a hand. Lee had one about a ghost fisherman that wandered the lake looking for his boat. Colby shared a story that he had read about werewolves. However, Ann's tale was the best.

Everyone was seated in a circle around the campfire. The flames of the fire highlighted Ann's red hair giving her a powerful presence. Her words came slowly and deliberately, drawing out each thought in a perfect, suspenseful pace. She could really tell a story, probably the reason why she wanted so desperately to be a journalist.

For hundreds of years, these dark woods have held a secret. Every living part of it knows the secret, from the top-most leaf on the tallest oak to the tiniest earthworm needling through the earth below. They see them. They hear them. They feel them. They fear them. They are forced to watch, with no way to stop them, no way to scream out.

"Who?" asked Theo, the youngest of the campers. His long bangs hung over his wide, puppy dog eyes. He was already sitting so far on the edge of a log that it looked as if he would tumble to the ground at any moment.

Not who, what. As the sun sets, the creatures of the forest see them creeping across the ground. The trees aren't swaying in the breeze; they're shuddering at the creatures' touch as they crawl slowly up their trunks. These things are dark; darker than the moonless night. And they are everywhere. They not only infect the woods where we are camping tonight, but many other forests across the entire globe. To humans, they look like normal , everyday shadows, yet the denizens of the woods know them as more. They know their true mission. They know what the creatures are looking for.

Ann shifted in her seat, providing an excuse for a dramatic pause. She sat back to see if her story was gaining traction with the boys. It was. They were all ears and eager for more. Not one of them stirred as the campfire crackled. They waited anxiously for her to continue.

Oh, I see, you want to know what they're looking for. That's easy. They only want one thing. They're looking for blood, human blood. The shadows latch onto their victims. They roll over the victims face, covering their mouth and nose. It's no use to fight or to gasp for breath. They will continue to hold until their victim loses consciousness. Then, this poor person is dragged across the woodland floor to a hiding place where the shadows leave them to find their next victim. If a victim should regain consciousness while the shadows are away, the unfortunate soul would still find himself lost in the shadows' hiding place deep in the woods, soon to be re-captured by the creatures. There is no hope.

I know this seems like a terrible fate, but you must understand we've only just begun this cautionary tale. For you see, the shadows are just errand boys. It's their master that is the real monster of the story. The shadows only attack during the full moon. The moon's glow gives them form. The shadows hunt and take victim after victim. Once they have collected enough bodies; they call their master, a beast that they have named Emperor. He is a monster that is very different from the shadows. He feeds off the blood from the humans that the lowly shadows have captured. In fact, when the shadows call their master, there's a celebration. Well, more like a wild party, where helpless folks are paraded before the Emperor.

Now, I know what you're thinking. This Emperor is not a vampire. He doesn't consume blood to survive. He does it because he wants to. He enjoys it. He loves it. He craves it like chocolate. And he, like others of his kind, is especially fond of the blood of leaders and important people; their blood is like a lip smacking delicacy.

Do you remember that I said that once you're in the clutches of a shadow, there's no hope? Well, there was an exception. It's a story about a girl who got away. It happened before we were even born. She was a teenager from Huntington.

Young Theo gulped, realizing that the city of Huntington, West Virginia, was just less than an hour from where they were now.

She was smart and beautiful. She was a born leader. You know the type; cheer captain and honor roll regular. In other words, she made the perfect dessert for the Emperor. She was camping in these very woods with her parents during the 4th of July weekend. She was a typical teenage girl, not too keen about sleeping in the dirt and bugs. So, her parents

147

decided to sleep under the stars and the full moon, allowing her to have the entire tent to herself. They were already fast asleep when she turned on her book light and began flipping through the pages of the most current bestseller. She was so focused on the novel that she didn't even notice the shadows growing around her until it was too late.

She woke up in the middle of a great party. There were sounds of laughter, music, and talking. She could tell that she was in a clearing at the top of a hill. A hollowed tree, towering more than twenty feet, burned in the center of a giant bonfire. The light that it emitted was so bright, that it took a long time for her eyes to adjust. But, once they did, she wished that she was still blinded. She didn't want to see that the guests to this party were not human.

These dark figures looked like mythical demons. She looked again and could see something large a few feet away. It was blocking her view. What is that, she wondered, as her eyes adjusted to the light provided by the overwhelming flames of the bonfire. Is it a log or a boulder? But no, she was horrified to realize that it was a grown man, awake but paralyzed, lying in a pool of his own blood. The only thing he could do was scream; which only thrilled the shadows more. Unable to look at the sinister celebration, the girl tried to move, but found that her ankles were bound. She looked up to see a man dressed in a black cloak seated in a chair. I'm saved she thought, until she realized that the legs of his chair straddled her legs, essentially penning her to the ground. He appeared to be cheering the creatures on only stopping to jokingly warn them to not play with his food.

Too distracted by the scene before him, he hadn't yet noticed that she was conscious. She gathered her fear and put it aside. She pulled her knees to her chest and with everything she had in her, kicked her captor's chair. It went tumbling toward the bonfire with the cloaked man landing squarely on his head. She bobbled to her feet. They were still bound together tightly at the ankles so she began to hop. She hopped like she was in a sack race for her life. She could hear the creatures screeching behind her. If she could make it to the slope, she could roll down and away. It was too steep for the monsters to follow. It was probably too steep for her to survive, but it was her only chance. There was hope just a few hops away.

The cloaked man jumped in front of her. His eyes glowed. He snarled at her and with inhuman speed and strength, spun her around. Holding her back to his chest with one arm, he lifted his other hand. As his wide sleeve fell, she could see his long, sharp fingernails. With the precision of a surgeon, he sliced into her upper arm and began to drink of her blood. He was delighted by her sweet taste, almost to the point of giddiness. He was so engrossed in savoring every drop of her blood, that he didn't notice that she had wriggled free from the bindings on her ankles. She jumped straight up and braced both feet on his thighs. Startled, he quit drinking and grabbed her arms. She mustered all her remaining strength and pushed off with her legs. The two toppled over, off balance, hitting the ground hard. He let go with the impact, just as she had prayed he would. As soon as she touched grass, she tucked her arms and began to roll. She hit the edge of the meadow and down the hill's treacherous slope. She rolled over downed branches and sharp rocks, until she reached the bottom and could no longer hear the Emperor's mad shrieking.

Let me just say that you should be thankful for the dark sky tonight. The shadows won't be hunting, but they'll be back soon, to stalk their prey under the light of the full moon.

When she finished, it was completely silent. Later, Jumper described it by saying that even the crickets were choked with fear. Then, everyone burst into hoots and applause. "100 watts will light up every inch of my little tent. I get it now," Colby chuckled to himself.

Deciding that there was no way to top it, the campers separated to retire to their sleeping bags. Jumper's Dad gave him permission to walk her back to the park office where she was meeting her parents. The path was not long, but there were no lamp posts. The quarter moon shone brightly above, creating an eerie, shimmering effect on the grass. Jumper grabbed his flashlight and the two started off hand-in-hand.

"That was some story, babe," Jumper remarked.

"Thanks Jump. I'm just so happy that I got to come tonight and see you."

"Yeah, about that, how did you talk your parents into driving you all this way just to spend a few hours with me? Did they have another reason to come all this way?"

"Oh, it's nothing. Trust me. Hey, I have to go to the little girls' room, so I'm gonna head into the park office. If my folks aren't in the parking lot when I'm done; I'll just wait inside with the rangers. Why don't you go ahead and start back?"

Jumper could see a couple of park rangers inside the office. "If you're sure?"

"Yeah."

"Well, okay." He gently brushed her hair away from her face and tucked it behind her ears. "It really did mean a lot to me that you showed up tonight. I love it that you scared the guys. You're a really cool chick." He kissed her goodnight and headed back up the trail.

She stood there thinking, a satisfied smile spread across her face. Who would have ever thought that Jumper Johnson could be so sweet? Maybe this would work. Maybe it wouldn't be a total disaster if he knew the truth. Once he was out of sight, she turned on her heel and her body began to fade out of sight. A sonic boom echoed through the woods. She was gone.

Chapter 19: The Guardian & The Charge

"Quiet, people," Mrs. Bethany instructed her study hall students.

As soon as her back was turned, Brooke took advantage. She reached up to massage Colby's shoulders. Without turning around, he patted her hand. She leaned up so that he could feel her cool breath on the back of his neck. He felt chills run to every inch of his body as she spoke.

"I would love to see you tonight. Can you come over to my house?"

Colby tensed. He knew perfectly well of the implications of Brooke's invitation. He had been there earlier this week, the night that Brooke's parents packed for their two-week trip to Europe. They left yesterday. He and Brooke would be alone. He was a good guy, but he was also a teenage boy. It didn't help that her voice washed over him like a sun-warmed ocean wave.

"I…uh…I," Colby struggled for the right words, or at the very least, *any* words.

"You're such a smooth operator. Be there at six, Coco Bear."

Colby must have dropped his pencil fifty times during class, then twenty more times in his next class. He couldn't stop fidgeting and it was only enhancing his already clumsy nature. When the final bell rang, he bolted for home. He couldn't walk with Keira today. She would know that something was up. What would he say? He didn't want to think about facing her now. He probably wouldn't have had to. It was a beautiful early summer day, so he supposed that she probably ditched her final few classes.

As a matter of fact, she had. As the last bell rang at school, Keira tiptoed barefoot across the creaky boardwalk at The Landing. She just wanted some time away. She needed time to forget and she always found it helpful to reconnect with nature. She hopped on top of the picnic table in the center of the shelterhouse and sprawled out on her back. She closed her eyes and concentrated on nothing but the sound of the river lapping against the bank. A tugboat and barge had passed moments before, leaving behind a wake that came crashing to shore. As the waves began to wane, she felt her tension wane too. It was quiet. Luckily, it was the middle of the afternoon. Since the local fishermen preferred early morning and late evening, The Landing was deserted, just the way she liked it. Well, almost the way she liked it. It would be better if Colby were there. She pulled her knees up and just sat there, savoring the quiet.

Colby arrived home, showered, and put on the expensive pair of jeans that Brooke had given him on his birthday. He changed his shirt a hundred times, but finally settled on a blue polo, remembering that she said she liked it because it brought out his eyes. It was the perfect medium, not too dressy or too casual. He would look good, but not seem like he was trying too hard. Just as he was putting the final touches on his hair, he heard the incessant honking from a car outside. It was his ride. He knew that tutoring the varsity basketball team would come in handy some day.

The guys dropped him off in front of Brooke's house at about ten after six. As he stepped from the car, the sky opened up and rain blew at him from all sides. The car pulled away from the curb with screeching tires and much whooping and hollering. Colby's face flushed as he realized that Brooke would probably hear it, even from inside the house. The rain's intensity pushed him up the steps to the front door. To his surprise, she was not there to greet him, but the arched double doors were wide open, swaying in the fierce wind. He stepped inside cautiously, closing them behind. He slipped off his wet jacket and hung it on the foyer's coat tree.

"Brooke, sorry I'm late. Where are you?"

"Help! Colby, help!"

He knew in an instant that it was Brooke. Without a moment's hesitation, he took the stairs three at a time to the second floor.

"Noooo!" she screamed.

He burst through her bedroom door.

Brooke was bent backwards toward an open window. The pure white window sheers were blowing wildly around her, forced by the winds of the oncoming storm. Her eyes were large with terror and her feet and hands bound. Perched on the window sash was a hideous mogdoc. One emaciated, clawed hand held a dagger to Brooke's throat; the other hand pinned her shoulder. Four other mogdocs stood at the ready in a line in front of Brooke.

The one holding Brooke spoke while the rest anxiously writhed and hissed, flicking their snakelike tongues. The tiny creature's voice was unexpectedly low and booming. "You sicken me, you filthy rodent. All that power and you bow to the humans, it is disgusting. You reek with the stench of humanity almost as much as you reek of guardian." He turned up his nose in revulsion. "Listen to me, guardian, you will bring your dark-haired charge to Emperor Gammen and he may let your pet live. You have until midnight."

The mogdoc on the left end broke flank and sprang into the air, catching the curtain rod with one hand and then dangling from it. His pulled back his free hand, claws extended. Then, he brought it down with force, slashing through reality itself, creating some sort of magical portal. The mogdoc holding Brooke captive went first, the others grabbed her legs as she was dragged through. The tear sealed itself after the last one managed its way through. All that remained was a thin, silver streak hanging in the air in front of the window.

"Gammen," Colby gasped. He pulled out his cell phone and dialed the only person that he knew could help.

155

Keira sat up with a start. She had fallen asleep on top of the picnic table in the shelterhouse at The Landing. She pulled her phone from her pocket.

"Hey-oh."

"I need your help."

"Colby, what's wrong?"

"Your bad guy...Gammen...he's kidnapped Brooke. I think that he thinks you're me. I mean, I'm you."

"What? Where are you?"

"Brooke's house, please hurry. I don't know what to do. Keira, you're the only one..."

"Don't worry, I'm coming with help."

***

Keira, Nana, August, and Bianca arrived at Brooke's home in less than ten minutes after the call. Colby led them upstairs and gave his detailed account of the kidnapping.

"He told me to bring my black-haired charge," Colby repeated. "He kept saying that I stunk like a guardian."

"Brainless hounds," August smirked. "They must have followed the scent. They've been watching, trying to figure out who's the guardian."

"They *are* together a lot, so their scents were mingled," Bianca added. "His on her, her's on him. They had to deduce which was which."

"And they chose Colby because he's so responsible," Keira offered.

"No," Colby said. "It's because of the coaster. If that mogdoc succeeded, their problems were over, if he failed, it would be the ultimate litmus test to find the guardian."

"And you passed the test by surrendering your own life to save me," Keira whispered. "And this is how I repay you, by putting your girlfriend's life at risk."

Colby hadn't thought of it that way. This was Gammen's fault, not Keira's. "You can't 'pass' a litmus test. Gee whiz, Keira, no wonder you're pulling a C in chemistry," he said in a feeble attempt to lighten the mood and alleviate her guilt.

She recognized and appreciated his effort. "Please, I'm just glad to see that you stayed conscious this time."

"That's enough," August interrupted. "Colby, do you recall how many of them were here?"

"Five, but I don't care. That's not important now. We're getting Brooke back. How do we get to Gammen? Can we make it by midnight?"

Keira then noticed that her father had taken a seat and was rubbing his temples. The realization hit her like a ton of bricks. She knew what her father surmised in only seconds. There were five. It had to be the Sect of Low, the emperor's best warriors.

"No!" Bianca spoke up. "I know what you're thinking, August, but we've given up too much to keep Keira safe. I'm not about to let her walk into Gammen's arms now."

August looked up, the weight of the world on his brow. "Bianca, dear, I think we have to let her go. This girl is a friend of Keira's, her human friend, her human gift. I think it's time. This is the perfect opportunity. He has this whole thing mixed up, so she's coming into it with a definite advantage. She's had combat training. She's ready."

"Please, August, no."

"We have a plan." August explained, "That's all we've been doing for the past three months. We've plotted out what we thought was every possible scenario. A hostage situation is certainly one of them, but I don't believe that the mogdocs have ever taken a regular human captive before. We didn't anticipate that they would think Colby was a guardian or that they would think the charge was old enough to be one of you. This indicates that they have little intel. They're pretty much flying blind, which is good for us. Regardless, we do have a plan to follow them. Nana, I need you to go back to the training room for some more weapons and contact our young friend, we'll need her help to re-open the threshold. Colby and Keira, prepare for battle."

"No," Keira said forcefully. "You can't expect Colby to fight. He is not going."

"Don't worry, sweetheart. He probably won't have to fight, but you had better tell Colby about your other special ability. You may need to use it to escape tonight and we can't risk your boyfriend going into shock and slowing us down."

"I'm/He's not her/my boyfriend!" the two said in unison.

Keira rolled her eyes and took Colby by the hand. She led him into the hallway and then to the room at the end. It appeared to be some sort of game room, with a massive billiards table in the center flanked by high tables with matching stools. A mahogany bar stretched across the end of the room with rows of glassware on shelves behind.

"What I'm about to tell you is very personal," Keira started. "Telling you this means that I have to trust you."

"It's a little late to have trust issues now, don't you think?"

"Maybe, first, tell me what you were doing here alone with Brooke tonight."

"I really like Brooke," he said. "She's my girlfriend. Let's leave it at that."

"Why did I ask?"

"Why did you? It's none of your business."

"Forget it. Let's just move on," she said. "You're gonna want to sit down."

Colby's patience ran out. "Do we really have time for this? My best friend's the tooth fairy and my girlfriend's been kidnapped by the boogeyman. I don't think there's much left that can shock me."

"Really? Well, I turn into a mouse."

She stood before Colby with her hands on her hips. He could see that she was completely serious.

"What do you mean…a mouse?"

"Mickey and Minnie. Stuart Little. Nothing was stirring, not even a…"

Colby was bewildered. This bit of information was just not sinking in. After an awkward moment of silence, Keira continued, "Remember the night that I told you about being a guardian. I said that in another part of the world they call us ratón de los dientes. That name translates to 'tooth mouse'. It's Spain's version of the tooth fairy. It turns out that they're a bit closer to the real story than the folks here in the states."

Colby struggled to understand. He could feel Keira's frustration pushing at him like a prosecuting attorney waiting for the defendant's response to a loaded question. He scrambled to think of the most sensitive way to respond.

"What kind of mouse?"

"Huh?" Keira said looking at him in utter disbelief. "Oh, I'm told that I'm a silky black with a twitchy nose and whiskers...very cute. After I save your girlfriend, maybe I can run the exercise wheel for you."

"I didn't mean..."

Keira closed her eyes and shook the stress from her body. "Sorry. It's just maddening, you know? You've had to put up with so much craziness from me. I was just trying to save you this one little thing. You must think that I'm a total freak."

Keira sat down beside Colby and buried her face in her hands. From behind them she mumbled, "This is my fault. If you had never known me, you wouldn't be in danger. Now I've put Brooke in danger too. She doesn't even know what I've gotten her into."

Keira looked up. "If something happens to you..." She left the rest unsaid and lowered her head.

"Hey, this mouse thing could be kinda cool," Colby said. "Can you change at will?"

Keira lifted her head and nodded. He was distracting her from her feelings again. This time it was a welcome distraction.

"Wow, if it were me, I'd be changing all the time."

"Once I change, it takes a while to change back. It really zaps my strength, so it's more of an emergency thing."

"So guardians probably have this ability in case they're caught in a charge's room?"

Keira nodded again, this time with a smile. "Thanks for understanding," she said, rising to her feet. "Enough of this, we've got a damsel in distress to save."

"Hold it a second. There's something I have to tell you."

Keira didn't ask, she just squinted at him, ready to take the worst.

"I know I don't have super powers like you, but sometimes I remember things."

"Sure, that's why you're the smartest kid at school." Keira couldn't fathom what this had to do with their upcoming mission.

"That's not what I mean. It's hard to explain. I guess I have a little bit of a photographic memory, but it's not always just memories. Like sometimes, I'll stare at a page in a book or when something good happens, I'll blink my eyes and try to freeze that image. It's like capturing a snapshot in my head."

"Okay," Keira encouraged, still not knowing where this was leading.

"Well, sometimes, I see pictures that I didn't 'take', something from the future. It doesn't happen often, but I vaguely remember seeing something the night of the dance last fall. I think it's important."

"Why?"

"It was you and you were wearing the same outfit that you have on now."

"Oh."

"I saw you surprise a man dressed in black with a knife. You had it hidden in your right sleeve by your wrist." He took her hand and pulled back her sleeve to show her the spot.

"I was wondering where to strap my dagger so that Gammen wouldn't notice. Thank you."

She said nothing more, even though she wanted to. This vision sounded like prophetic sight. It also sounded like he had more than the one vision. Perhaps he inherited some of his ancestor's abilities. She could ask Nana about it later. For now, it was probably safer if no one knew.

Chapter 20: Ready

Colby was standing at the window when Nana returned. He watched her park and rush out of the car. She opened a huge red umbrella and balanced it against her shoulder to free her hands. She then pulled a worn duffel bag from the trunk, presumably full of weapons. The unrelenting thunderstorm harshly beat down on her the whole while.

Colby was about to head outside to help her when he noticed that she was not alone. A slender, woman wrapped in a white, hooded cloak stepped from the passenger side of the car. The rain didn't seem to affect the odd stranger. The drops fell around her, but not on her. She moved quickly, her cloak flowing gracefully around her. She almost seemed to float. Colby found himself frozen at the window, mystified by the stranger. He moved to the hallway as the two entered the house and started to the second floor. Nana topped the stairs first.

"Colby, dear, if you would," she requested as she handed him the heavy bag. He took the bag and immediately dropped it.

"Colby Hayes, you're the last person in the world that I'd expect to see caught up in this," said the lady in white.

Colby froze.

Keira pushed past him. "Ann, I'm so glad you can help us."

"Mogdocs suck. I'll do what I can," she replied.

"Traveler," Keira replied to Colby's unasked question. "Hey, don't blame me. It wasn't my secret to tell."

"Traveler?"

"I can teleport myself at will to almost any place or time," Ann explained as easily as if it were an afterschool job. "I can also open travel portals or in this case, re-open them."

"...and Jumper?" he questioned.

"Jump's kind of spirit...it's super, but all natural," Ann smiled. "And, btw, he doesn't know about any of this yet, it's a fairly recent development. So, let's keep this under wraps for a bit longer until I figure out if I'm going to tell him."

Colby nodded in agreement and a bit of disbelief. He moved back into the bedroom to hand off the duffel bag of weapons that Nana delivered.

August grabbed it from him with one hand and dumped the weapons onto the floor. Colby didn't appreciate the gesture, as he had just finished picking them up from the floor in the hallway, but he felt it best not to protest. August strapped a sword to one side and a gun to the other. Colby picked up a crossbow and flung it over his back.

"Do you know how to use that thing?" August asked him.

"I spent six years in 4-H Shooting Sports. I've got it covered," Colby replied.

"Humans!" August chuckled to himself. "And while we're on the subject, there's something that you'll need for our trip."

He beckoned Bianca to join them. As she approached, she slipped a silver bracelet off her wrist. She cupped Colby's hand and carefully handed him the trinket. On the end of the chain was what looked to be a smashed penny. "The mogdocs created this threshold, so we can't be sure of where it leads. If it passes through the barrier, you will need this. Hide it. If Gammen sees it, he'll know that you're human."

Human, the word triggered an epiphany. "It was you," he whispered.

Bianca knew immediately what he meant, but allowed him to talk his way through it.

"A long time ago, Ann told us a story, a scary story about a girl. This girl was the only one to escape the shadows and their master. I had already put it together that the master was one of the Gammens, but the girl was you, wasn't it? That's why you're not going with us."

She kissed him on the cheek and whispered "Just make sure that BOTH you and Brooke hold it when you come back. Good luck". The dainty bracelet was much too small for his wrist. He finally fastened it around his belt, tucking the coin into his waistband.

Meanwhile, down the hall, Nana pulled Keira aside for some last minute advice. Nana's face was sober. Keira could see that her mentor was carefully choosing her words in her head before her mouth even opened.

Nana began slowly, "Keira, your parents are optimistic, but as your teacher, I know that it is better to be prepared."

"Sure."

"I've been thinking about the prophecy and about what has transpired. Prophecies are not clear, precise statements. They are subject to interpretation. This one says 'impart a human gift'. Your parents, they first assumed that the gift would be an action or heirloom given willfully by a member of the Hayes family. Now, of course, they believe that the human gift is actually a human, Colby's friend."

"You don't?"

"Keira, gifts are given. The Banes girl was taken. There is a difference. In light of all that's happened, I fear that it may be someone else."

"Who else could it be?"

Nana's words were slow, each syllable deliberate so that Keira could feel the full weight of what was being said. "Keira, my dearest Keira, the word 'gift' can also mean 'sacrifice'."

"That thought crossed my mind too. But Nana, you have to know that I won't sacrifice Brooke or little Drew to defeat Gammen."

Nana grimaced, realizing that Keira did not comprehend the full extent of her words. "Keira, you have to realize that you may not have a choice."

Keira glared at Nana.

"...and the human to be sacrificed may be the one that's closest to you."

"Everyone. Here. Now!"

August's order vibrated in every corner of the mansion. Colby didn't even see her at first, but Ann was standing at the window in Brooke's bedroom. She had pulled t he hood of her cloak up to cover her curly, red hair. The long white cloak made her almost disappear in the white bedroom. Ann and August were holding their hands with palms forward and fingers spread, controlling a silver-bordered tear in reality that stretched from the white carpet to the white ceiling.

"Step in front of me," Ann ordered.

As Keira and Colby moved in front of her, she touched her inner wrist to each of their foreheads. Her white cloak swirled around her. As she began to concentrate her eyes clouded over so that they were completely white. As she touched each forehead with her wrist, there was a flash of light followed by a loud pop.

"I've marked each of you so that I can move you if you need my help."

Her voice was eerie. At least, that's what Colby thought at first. Then he realized that it wasn't different at all. The eerie part was that her voice was still Ann's voice, even though she looked so other-worldly. He assumed that she would sound different; that she would be different. "Move us how?" he asked.

Keira stepped in. "Ann's a traveler. She can travel through time and space. She's placed her mark on us so that she can use it, kind of like a homing beacon, to locate us and move us to safety if we get in trouble."

"That's right," she confirmed. "And I've marked your Dad since he's going too. Plus, I've marked this." She tossed a ring from Brooke's jewelry box to Keira. "Just get close to Brooke and slip it to her. I'll use it to bring her back safely too."

"Have you ever done this before?" Keira asked. She had read about the mark during her training, but it was something that was only attempted by highly experienced travelers.

"Don't get me wrong. It's definitely a last resort, but it should work. I've covered all the basics."

"How will you keep from pulling us out too early?" Colby asked.

Keira interjected. "Mom will know if something's wrong."

"That's right. Her Mom and Dad's bond is very strong. Bianca will know if something goes wrong. If she senses trouble, I will use the mark to pull you back immediately."

Nana inspected the invisible mark on Keira's forehead and took her position beside Ann. "Please be careful. I would very much like for you to join me for my birthday party next month," she said to August.

"You old fox, I would never miss your 500th," August smiled. He kissed her on the cheek and turned to the others.

"Here's the plan. Ann and Nana will stay here and keep the threshold open for our return. Bianca, stay here and alert them if there's trouble. Besides, Gammen would love nothing better than to get his claws on you. The rest of us will go through. I do all the talking. Play into the roles that they've given you. We'll pretend to exchange Keira for Brooke. When Brooke is clear, Colby will escape back he way we came. Keira, they think you're human, they won't expect your speed and strength. Bov only keeps one or two guards, if even that many, with him. He's so paranoid that he doesn't even trust his own guards and so egotistical that he thinks he doesn't need them. Let's hope the Sect isn't there, but just in case." He pulled a new dagger from its sheath and presented it to Keira. "Be careful with this one. It's tipped with a special poison, lethal to non-humans."

"What about humans?" Colby asked.

"You could lick it like leftover cake batter on your mom's wooden spoon."

"August, this is much too dangerous." Bianca pleaded.

Colby noticed a flash of excitement on August's face and grinned back. It was evident that Keira inherited her love of adventure from her father. Colby couldn't help but think that August probably enjoyed the excitement that this mission offered, a real deviation from his regular life.

August captured Colby's returning grin and called him out. "Colby, don't misunderstand. She's right, this situation is grave. The mogdocs that you saw, the Sect of Low, they are lightning fast, vicious, and merciless. Emperor Gammen, himself, is one of the most formidable beings alive. When it's time, don't look back. Run straight through the tear. No matter what."

"Yes, sir," Colby replied with genuine admiration.

"Ready!" said August standing before the rest, facing the threshold.

"Ready!" Colby replied.

"Ready, Dad!" Keira returned.

The word 'Dad' flowed more easily from her tongue that it had before. Keira said it without even thinking and it didn't go unnoticed. August took her hand in his. "Be smart and careful. Know that I will never leave you."

He kissed her on the forehead. Then, the three stepped hand-in-hand through the ragged, silver tear in reality.

Chapter 21: Until Midnight

Colby gripped the token, held his breath, and closed his eyes as they stepped forward. He felt the gust of wind bash his face. At first he thought it was just part of passing through the tear, but when the wind didn't stop he opened his eyes to see that they were standing on the roof of a skyscraper. He remembered this place from a book. School, of course, that's where his true talent soared. A nearly photographic memory served him well in his academic pursuits. That's what he offered to this team now.

"Where are we?" August asked taking a protective stance in front of Kiera and Colby.

"We haven't crossed the barrier." Colby said with a sideways glance to Keira, "It's Dubai. I recognize it from our Geography book. Over there, the building that looks like a sailboat, that's the Burj Al Arab. And then over there in the water, you can see one of the Palm islands."

"Dubai, that's in the Middle East, right?" Keira asked.

Colby nodded in the affirmative.

"It's 11:45," Colby noted by his watch under Dubai's bright morning sun. "I hope that he meant midnight, our time. Why does it have to be so close? How long till we get to Bov?"

"That's Emperor Gammen to you," boomed a voice from behind them.

They pivoted to see the great Bov Gammen in a ceremonial, black hooded cloak with tribal beads and black feathers hanging from the neck. He appeared to be roughly the same height as August, as opposed to the three foot, average mogdoc that crouched at Gammen's left side as if ready to pounce. The Emperor's skin, including his face, was completely covered.

A rolling office chair was positioned behind the Emperor. Brooke sat there defeated and gagged. Her arms were lashed loosely at the wrists to the armrests. Her feet were bound together. A mogdoc flanked her at each position; north, south, east, and west. Even in her desperate state, she managed to lift her head at their approach.

"August, what a lovely surprise," Gammen snarled. Of course, he was not at all surprised to see him.

August showed absolutely no emotion. If Colby hadn't known better, he would have thought that Mr. Ryan was bored. "There is no need for niceties, Emperor. We are here for a fair exchange, his charge for your hostage."

"You know, August, I thought your young one would prove to be more of a challenge. Yet, here you are, bringing him and his charge right to my doorstep. What service!"

"What did you do with Bobby?" Colby demanded. August held his hand in front of Colby's chest in warning.

"No August, it is a fair question. Listen to me, boy, you may sympathize with these weak creatures, but you will find no tolerance for them here. A master of sport and a master of science, both receiving assistance from you, it only seemed logical that one may be your charge. Of course, the girl slipped through my fingers, but that is of no consequence."

"The boy, what did you do with the boy?"

"The boy was not a charge, so he was of no use to me."

"He means to say that Bobby is dead," August whispered to Colby. Gammen laughed madly at the sight of Colby's disgust.

"Odd," started Gammen. "Your progeny should have known better than to tie himself emotionally to such frail creatures. He made it only too easy. But, I guess the apple doesn't fall far from the tree." He smiled widely showing off an intimidating pair of fangs. "How's your delicate Bianca? She tasted so delicious last time we met."

August sneered and stepped in front of Colby. "Do we have a deal?"

"Always a pleasure, August," Gammen laughed and snapped his fingers. "You first."

The mogdoc warrior at Gammen's side responded to the nonverbal cue. He moved toward Keira. Keeping to her role, Keira put up a weak fight. The mogdoc brought her to the Emperor's side. Both of them kept their eyes on August. So, it was easy for Keira to slip the ring under her boot.

"Now you," August demanded.

Emperor Gammen pulled back his hood and clutched Keira to bring her closer. "I don't think so. I also seek the child of sun and moon. Thank you for bringing him to me."

The hood of his cloak fell as he threw back his head in an over-dramatized maniacal laugh. Everyone's eyes were on the supreme evil leader. Colby was dumbfounded. The Emperor was human. Actually, he just *looked* human. Colby felt a sudden pang of déjà vu. He saw something familiar in Gammen's face, but could not place it. The Emperor caught notice of Colby's gaze and glared back at him.

Keira made use of the distraction to drop the ring and kick it back to Brooke with her right foot. At the same time, she pulled the poisoned dagger from its concealed sheath at her right wrist. She thrust it forward. Gammen blocked and in retaliation, shoved her into the roof access door with tremendous strength. The heavy, steel door bent under the force. Keira's body lay limp at its base.

"Noooo!," howled Colby.

"Go now!" August ordered. "I'll get the girls."

Gammen knelt beside Keira's motionless body and pulled the dagger from her hand. The mogdoc guard moved into position between his master and August. "Dead! Dead! Death has marked you all!" it screeched in pure joy.

Colby pulled the crossbow from his back and took aim on the howling mogdoc. His first shot was short, dropping before it reached its target. The creature stormed at him, but he was ready. His second shot was perfect, straight into its abdomen. The force of the arrow pushed the fiend back through the air, just preventing his claws from reaching Colby. It fell and writhed in pain. Colby knelt over the creature and stabbed it again with his last arrow, a death blow to the heart.

Colby looked up just in time to see the steel lock into his bicep. A sharp pang ensued and he dropped the crossbow. "Aaahh!" he screamed as he pulled the dagger from his arm. He lifted it weakly and lunged at Gammen. The Emperor caught his wrist and yanked his arm high into the air. The copper token pulled out of his waistband and clinked against the bracelet chain. There it dangled from his belt in plain view.

"You're the charge! How delightful," Gammen laughed. His joy reflected in his eyes. "Let's see if your guardian can protect you on my side of the barrier."

Gammen slashed a new rip in space with one clawed hand while he grasped Colby in the other. "Bring the girl," he ordered as he dragged Colby through the barrier. August, now kneeling beside his daughter's broken body, looked to Colby with regret.

Colby was too scared to close his eyes this time. The little light from the city rooftop flashed and was suddenly gone. When his eyes adjusted, he could see that he was now in a gigantic underground cavern. Torches lined each side of the room. An underground lake took up three quarters of the room. The smell of must and decay filled the chamber. The floor was thick with mud. "Muddy footprints," Colby thought aloud.

The remaining members of the Sect of Low followed, each with one hand supporting Brooke's chair and the other hand securing her arms, as if she could get away. They quickly re-tied her to a pole planted at the water's edge. They resumed their guard positions; north, east, west and south.

"Gammen!"

The Emperor yanked Colby around to see August standing at the threshold.

"My, my, you are persistent," the emperor hissed. "I was so sure it was the boy, but no, a girl. You thought a little girl, *your* little girl, would stop me."

"*I'LL* stop you." August moved toward him pulling a sword from its sheath on his back.

Using a single hand, Gammen flung Colby onto the cavern floor. Mud splattered around him when he hit the ground.

"You will try," Gammen sneered as he lifted the stolen, poisoned dagger.

Their blades clashed with such force that sparks flashed across the dark cavern. Gammen was slightly more skilled as a swordsman, but August's agility made up the difference. Their steel blades met over and over. The mogdocs did not move from Brooke. They grunted and jeered at the display of strength before them until Brooke screamed out. Distracted, August dropped his guard. Gammen took advantage and lashed out with his claws, slicing August's neck from chin to clavicle. He cried out and dropped to his knees, clutching his neck. Gammen used the dagger to fling the sword out of his hands.

Blood poured from August's wounds. Brooke, just a few feet away, struggled against her ropes, behind the circle of mogdoc elite.

Gammen leaned over the weakened August, dagger still in hand. "Your prophecy dies today."

"Not today," Colby said as he plunged August's sword into Gammen's back.

"Yes, today," Gammen said smiling. He did not even bother to dislodge the sword from his back before shoving Colby into the air with a mere flick of his wrist. Colby soared across the cavern, falling into the murky waters of the underground lake. Gammen turned his attention back to August. He placed one hand behind August's head and lifted it. The poisoned dagger was still in Gammen's possession. August closed his eyes as Gammen pulled back the dagger to deliver the final blow.

"Let him go. It's me that you want," said a weak voice from the threshold.

"So true, little girl. Don't worry; you will also taste death at the tip of my dagger."

His left hand still supporting August's head, he pulled back the dagger again. However, as he thrust it down, the air around August shimmered and in the final second, his transformation was complete. It was a second that came just in time for August; a second too early for Gammen. Where the injured father once laid, a gray mouse scurried away. And with his intended target gone, Gammen plunged the poisoned dagger into his own hand.

The Emperor cried out in pain. He was so focused on his hand that he did not see Keira until her boot was in his face. She kicked so hard that he flipped head over heels and his back hit the cavern floor. She picked up the dagger and held it to Gammen's throat. "It's done," Keira said and thrust the dagger into his chest.

She jumped as a drenched Colby splashed behind her and pulled himself onto the wet cavern floor. Keira yanked the dagger from Gammen's dying body and swiftly moved to Colby's side, stopping only to gently pick up an injured, gray mouse and place him in the big front pocket of her hoodie. She arrived at Colby's side for support. He clumsily draped over her shoulder. She looked into his eyes, but his sights were set beyond her. "Brooke!"

The poison had moved very slowly. Gammen used the extra time to drag his unresponsive torso across the cavern floor to the hostage's pole. The four mogdocs, still in their positions, were now bowing. The Emperor was bleeding heavily as the poison worked its way through his body. Though fatally wounded, he pushed himself to his knees. With a painful groan, he reached up to the ropes cutting into Brooke's wrists and loosened them quickly with his claws, allowing her to fall forward.

He softly kissed her cheek and with his last breath he turned and screamed at his enemies, "The House of Gammen rules forever! Long live Broo Gammen, Empress of the Mogdoc Empire!"

Brooke rose, letting her father fall to the ground. She smirked then she lifted a well-manicured finger and elegantly sliced a tear in the space before her. She and the remaining four members of the Sect of Low vanished into the rip as her father took his last breath.

Colby suddenly felt light-headed and dizzy. He lifted his hand. It was transparent. He looked to

Keira as she faded away behind an amplified sonic
boom.

Chapter 22: Going Places

"Get up! Get up, Colby!"

Colby shook the fog from his head and teetered to his feet. "My head...Where are we?"

"Looks like Ann needs more practice. We're definitely not back at Brooke's house."

"Brooke," Colby sighed. His legs gave way. He knelt on the ground and lowered his head.

Keira didn't know what to say or even what to feel. She couldn't believe that she had been tricked, but she found herself filled with relief from the guilt she had assumed when she blamed herself for Brooke's capture. She shook it off. Now was not the time to dwell on feelings. They were still in danger.

Keira started to look around to get her bearings. From under the tall spike-leafed trees and vines which surrounded them, she couldn't see any buildings. In fact, there was not a single sign of civilization. The heat was suppressing. Sweat ran down her forehead and dripped off the tip of her nose. She took the mouse from her front pocket and set him gently on a rotting stump. "Dad, I wish you could tell me what to do." The mouse looked up at her and twitched his nose in sympathy.

She pulled off her hoodie to expose the white t-shirt beneath. "It looks like we're in the rain forest. Do you think we're in South America?" She asked as she picked the mouse up to begin making her way through the dense undergrowth.

"Could be," Colby said hesitantly. He rubbed his eyes and stood up.

"It's going to be okay."

"Yeah, I know. Listen, I don't want to…" Something distracted him. His eyes dropped to the ground to examine an impression in the earth. "Maybe it's the Galapagos Islands. These tracks look like they've been made by a big lizard. I'm guessing a komodo dragon."

Click. Click.

The clicking noise gave way to a purr that slowly turned into a hiss as a six-foot lizard stepped from the undergrowth.

"Definitely not a komodo dragon," Keira gulped from behind him. "Run!"

Colby stumbled and Keira grabbed him by his shirt with her free hand. Her strength surprised him. She put him back on his feet without stopping. He took his first full stride and was surprised when his foot didn't touch the ground. He reached for Keira, but she was already gone.

Keira was relieved to feel concrete below her feet this time. Her Dad, the mouse, scurried up her arm to sit on her shoulder. He had already begun healing. Colby was on his knees, too dizzy to stand, not more than three feet away. She could hear voices on the other side of the block wall in front of them.

"Let's see if your guardian can protect you on my side of the barrier," she heard.

They were back on the rooftop in Dubai, sometime before the time they left. Keira moved silently around the wall to see Gammen dragging a second Colby through the tear in space to the underground cavern, just as he had moments before. She looked down. Just around the corner, her body lay lifeless at the base of the roof access door. Her Dad was weeping over it.

"Bring the girl," Gammen ordered.

Keira watched quietly as the Sect carried Brooke through the barrier. They didn't carry her like a hostage. They carried her with respect and care. They carried the rolling office chair up high like it was a traveling throne. Why didn't she see it before? She couldn't help but feel completely naïve. However, she didn't have time to dwell on that thought now. Her other self had awakened and August was rising to follow Gammen. She had to warn him about Brooke, rather Broo.

"You have got to be kidding me!"

Keira jerked around to see Brooke standing behind her. Her green eyes were blazing. She was cussing and pulling prehistoric fern leaves from her hair. Keira had forgotten about the ring. She had slipped it to Brooke for her rescue which meant that she still had it and Ann was targeting it just like the marks on Keira, August, and Colby.

"You know, your little tricks change nothing. I am still Empress and I have you and your Daddy to thank for that." She tossed her ring at Keira's head. "And you ruined my favorite ring!"

Keira caught it and turned her back on Broo. "Dad!" she yelled, but it was too late. The August from the past had already crossed the barrier into the underground cavern. She could see the left foot of her other self disappear into the tear. Keira turned back to Broo who was still fuming.

"What do you want?"

Broo stopped muttering curses under her breath. She stared eerily at Keira. "Don't you know? I want everything," Broo laughed. "And I'll start with your gift." She glanced down at Colby.

"Colby? You think Colby is a gift? No way! Have you even read the prophecy? You have no idea what you're talking about. You're wrong like...."

"Stop babbling, stupid rat. You will address me as High Empress Gammen, Ruler of the Mogdoc Empire."

She circled Keira, studying her with probing green eyes.

"You know, Keira, I never liked you, but I didn't realize that it was because you were a plague-spreading trash eater."

Broo laughed with a crazed hysteria, a talent that she had unmistakably inherited from her father. Keira felt the hairs on the back of her neck prick up, but she stood silent, waiting for her moment. Broo continued circling. "So, are you saying that he is not your charge, or, are you saying that he is not the human gift?" She gave Keira a moment to respond, but Keira lifted her chin and didn't speak.

"From your silence, I'm guessing you mean that *you* really aren't the prophesied, perfect one. Yeah, I don't blame you. That really is very, very hard to believe. I mean, you, the prodigal hero, the guardian savior. Really, Keira, you aren't fooling anyone."

Colby could only read the last word 'anyone' from her lips, but nothing more. His ears were still ringing from the sonic boom of the last trip. He looked at them, desperately trying to regain his balance so that he could come to Keira's aid. His normal clumsiness did not help his current situation.

Broo looked him up and down before continuing her lecture to Keira. "No, I believe that you are lying to protect my little, Coco Bear."

That was the last straw. Keira stepped in front of Broo so that her circling came to an abrupt halt. They were so close that their noses nearly touched. "He is not what you're looking for and if you touch him…"

"If I touch him again, you mean?"

In a rage, Keira grabbed Broo's neck and squeezed. She had never wished harm on another creature in all her life, that is, she had never until this moment. She shook Broo back and forth as she squeezed, flopping her head forward and back. She grasped Broo's life in her hands. She could end it. She had the strength to end it right now. She could if she were that kind of person, but she wasn't. In shock, she pulled back her hands and threw them in the air.

Before Keira could make another move or even say a word. Those menacing green eyes made her regret releasing her grip. "Remember with whom you are dealing," Broo growled.

Broo's voice was much lower than before. Surprised, Keira stepped back as Broo started to grow. Her black satin nightgown bulged and finally burst open in a fury of fur and muscle. Keira fell back from the force of the change as Broo sprang forward as a full werewolf.

Keira scrambled backwards to Colby. She pulled on his shirt screaming, "Colby! Get up! Dad!"

The mouse scampered across the top of the low wall, ushering the way to escape. Keira grabbed Colby up and pulled him, following her father toward the tear leading back to Brooke's bedroom. The wolf snarled and lunged at them. She edged closer and closer, nipping at her heels. Keira threw Colby through the threshold. Colby and the mouse landed in the white bedroom, knocking over Nana and Ann in the process. As they fell to the floor the tear collapsed, but not before they heard the chilling howl of the wolf.

The threshold closed just as Keira bound into it. Instead of landing on the soft, white bedroom carpet, she crashed into the concrete half wall that protected the roof's edge. Keira was trapped. Behind her was a fall to her death. In front of her was the wolf. Broo was bearing her teeth and growling, relishing her inevitable triumph.

"You can't get him now. He's protected and he knows what you really are," Keira yelled as she edged along the wall.

The beast growled louder. The rooftop trembled. Keira covered her ears.

She braced herself against the short wall, her strength failing. The pain from her wounds started to set in. There was no Plan B. There was no way out. "What are you waiting for? Come and get me," she screamed.

Broo pounced on her. Keira fell on her back under the brute force. The werewolf mauled her torso, ripping into her back with her claws. She bit down on Keira's upper arm. Her incisors cut deep into the muscle. Pain shot through Keira's entire body. She screamed out. The wolf licked her lips to savor the taste of the surprisingly sweet blood of the half guardian. Fighting to the end, Keira fisted her unhurt arm and punched the wolf in the jaw. It was not enough.

Broo lifted her majestic head and howled. However, the celebratory howl was cut short with a sudden yelp and whimper. Then, like a naughty puppy, the wolf was lifted up by the scruff of her neck.

Keira crawled out from where she had been pinned. She grabbed her injured arm. Blood poured from the bite wound. She could feel the wetness from the blood seeping from her back as well. She felt weak and lightheaded. She was losing blood and very close to passing out. As Keira fought back the darkness that tried to close her heavy eyes, she looked up. Broo had phased back into her human form.

Then she saw him. Keira's mind was foggy from the attack, but she knew she wasn't dreaming. "William?"

The hand that had gripped the scruff of the wolf's neck now clutched Broo's long, blonde human hair. She reached back, scratching her captor's hands and screaming. "Don't stop me, Brun. You will regret this," Broo screeched in warning.

"You will not take her life. Not today. The empire is mine now. Keira is off limits."

He lifted his hand, gracefully tore a rip in space and shoved his sister through.

Chapter 23: On the Other Side

Colby rubbed his eyes, the mouse nibbled on his nose, urging him into action. "Keira!" Colby yelled.

Ann was in position. She had already begun work to re-open the threshold. A gleam of light started to trickle through the tear. Colby ran through it and slid on his knees beside Keira. She was alone on the rooftop, lying in a pool of her own blood. He lifted her motionless body and hurried back to her waiting family.

"Are they coming after you? Where's Brooke?" Bianca rushed to her daughter.

Keira lay limply in Colby's arms. She was now barely awake, deadly silent, and as pale as a ghost. Her clothes were soaked with dark, red blood. "Are Colby and Dad safe?"

"Yes, sweetheart, thanks to you," her mother answered.

Keira smiled softly and closed her eyes. As she fell back into unconsciousness, Bianca helped Colby ease her onto the bed.

Colby turned to address everyone. "Gammen's dead," he said. "Brooke...Brooke...," he gasped. He suddenly found it hard to breathe and couldn't speak. He closed his eyes and let his knees fall to the floor in grief.

Nana and Ann looked at each other. With silent resolve, they worked quickly to completely seal the spot of the tear. Bianca had just finished dressing Keira's wounds by the time Colby found composure. He rose to his feet and put a hand on Bianca's shoulder. "We have to leave here now. It's not safe. The new leader knows where we are."

"It's all right, Colby. We've sealed the threshold, so they can't follow you," Ann expelled in an effort to put everyone at ease.

"They won't need it. She'll know exactly where we are."

Bianca and Ann's faces reflected their complete confusion. However, Nana instantly put it all together. "Brooke. Where is Brooke?" she demanded.

Colby didn't answer, but he didn't need to. Nana could see the answer in his face.

"Am I to understand that the new empress would call this home?" she assumed aloud for everyone's benefit. He nodded in the affirmative.

Colby could hear the whisper of comprehension break from Ann's lips. "Brooke," she gasped. "I can get us out of here fast."

"It's too unpredictable. Let me take care of this."

Colby picked up Keira's unconscious body and led everyone, including the mouse, down the stairs and out the giant arched double doors.

***

Keira survived the confrontation with two broken ribs, a cut and broken arm, a fractured collarbone, a mild concussion, dozens of bruises, and four deep gashes across her back made from the claws of a werewolf. However, there was no need for casts or slings. Fast healing was a definite benefit of being a guardian.

Still, she required some time out of school for recovery. The official story was that she had crashed her four-wheeler in the woods. August volunteered to take the ATV out to create the evidence. He brought it back with mud up to the handlebars, twigs sticking out of every opening, and the biggest grin across his face.

Ann delivered homework assignments daily. Jumper always accompanied her and kept them entertained with widely exaggerated commentaries on the events of Keira's missed school days. Colby couldn't help but wonder about Jumper's reaction to the information that Ann would one day share with him. Would he take it as well as Colby did when he found out that Keira was a guardian? Did Colby take it well? He thought so.

Colby was at Keira's bedside the entire time, working to put all the pieces together. The guilt of his negligence weighed heavy on him. How could he have fallen so completely for Brooke? It felt so real.

Of course, Keira offered her own explanation on Brooke's hold over him. She said that there had always been rumors that Gammen could control the emotions of humans to make them do as he pleased. It made sense that this trait was passed on to his daughter. It made sense. Thinking back, Colby realized that he had been overcome by emotion whenever he was in Brooke's presence, especially when she leaned in close to speak to him and her breath touched his skin. Those moments he used to treasure. Now, they were forever ruined by her betrayal.

Everything about Mr. Banes came rushing back to Colby's mind. The comment he made about Colby's scent during their first meeting was at the forefront of those recollections. The thought sent chills down his spine. Colby remembered how Mr. Banes was completely uninterested in him until Brooke said something about him being special, then, and only then, he was suddenly engaged. He didn't look the same in the cavern, but there were still traces of Mr. Banes' face, his eyes, in the human form that Gammen chose for his final battle.

And he had now come to some other conclusions too.

He had only met Brooke at freshman orientation and was ready to ask her out on the first day of school. Of course, he had attributed his unusual boldness to the start of his freshman year. Now, it was clear that he was under her spell from the start.

She had marked him with that emerald medallion at the Halloween Bash. That thing roaming the party must have been a mogdoc. Poor Shara, tormented for having bad taste in accessories.

He recalled his conversation with Brooke on the night of the Fall Ball. It wasn't the roller coaster incident that led Gammen to believe that Colby was the guardian. It was what Colby, himself, had said to Brooke. She asked him flatly if he always protected Keira and he had told her that it was practically his job.

The roller coaster was a new revelation in itself. Brooke did duck out of line because she was afraid of the coaster; especially since she knew that it was a death trap. She got out of there because she knew what was about to happen. It must have been so difficult for her to muster all that fake concern when he and Keira reached the ground alive.

Lastly, he wondered how he missed those green eyes...mogdoc eyes. How could he have gazed in them so deeply and not see what was behind them. The increasing list of missed details made Colby feel like a complete idiot. Of course, hindsight is 20/20; Colby knew this. He knew that it wasn't his fault. The trouble was that his head knew it. His heart just knew the guilt of not seeing through the con. These were the thoughts that plagued Colby at Keira's bedside.

His best friend the hero...his girlfriend the villain. He felt like his loyalties had been in a tug-of-war for so long and then suddenly one side dropped its end. Now, he was left wallowing in the mud.

On the fourth day of Keira's recuperation, Ann arrived alone. As always, she found Colby sitting in Keira's room.

"Can we talk outside for a minute?" she asked.

He rose from his station and followed her to the kitchen and then out the back door. Nana was doing dishes in the kitchen sink and looked up briefly as they passed, then continued with her work.

The back door led to a well manicured, but small, backyard separated from the nearby freshly planted fields by a tall, plank board perimeter fence. It was a bright, early summer afternoon. They walked in silence to the far corner where a grand, old maple tree stood. Its branches held a bounty of broad leaves that shaded the spot nicely. Ann parked herself in the wooden swing supported by one of the tree's widest limbs. Colby leaned on the tree's thick trunk, arms folded. His eyes were focused on Ann.

Without prompting, she began her story.

"Fifteen years ago, a very special baby was born of sun and moon."

"Right," Colby interrupted. "I already understand. You've all got super powers. Do we really need to talk about this right now? I shouldn't leave Keira alone…"

Ann forced a smile. "You better listen. I don't have much time."

Colby let out a frustrated sigh and knelt down to sit cross-legged on the warm grass to the side of the swing.

"Okay, of sun and moon…anyway… there are many who believed that this baby would grow to become a great warrior and overcome the Mogdoc Empire."

"And this baby is you?"

"No, but many believe it is Keira. So, as a baby, she was hidden among humans where she could be educated and trained in safety, until it was time."

Colby was a bit surprised by the answer, but found it easily justified based on the events of the last few months.

Ann continued, "Her parents gave her up to conceal her identity. Since they couldn't be with her, they provided her with many protectors. I only know three of them. I don't know if Keira even knows who all of them are. Nana, of course, is her primary trainer and protection. Two travelers, my parents, also pledged to protect her, but now their pledge has fallen to my sister and me."

"Katie's only ten years old."

"That's not the point."

"Well, I guess it's good to know that you're watching out for her. It makes me feel so much better that she has someone besides a little old lady to protect her. You know, like a real defender with special abilities."

"That's only part of what I need to tell you. There's more," she continued. "Keira has a duty to perform to bring about the end of Broo, er Brooke, well, the whole mogdoc empire." She paused a moment to gauge his reaction to her using the B-word. She couldn't recall which name she should use at this time.

"Colby, these creatures are so cruel. If you only knew the pain and inhumanity that they've caused." She started to choke and paused to compose herself. "Their wickedness is so unrelenting that it also affects the human world, manifesting in the worst kind of evil. Keira must fulfill the master plan at all costs."

"Yes, I know, it's her destiny."

"No, Colby, there is no such thing as destiny. This is her calling. I don't mean to sound too corny, but she is the hope of all generations. When she succeeds, she will save both our worlds. So, listen to me carefully. If you try to stop her, I'll have no choice but to stop *you*."

"Why would I stop her?"

"Colby, just listen to what I'm telling you. Keira and her mission come first, before any connection that we have. My whole world depends on it. This isn't going to be easy and she will have to make some tough choices."

"Why would I stop her?" he repeated.

"Just see that you don't. I must trust that you will listen to me and never forget this conversation," Ann said as she planted her feet back on the ground. "And Colby, one more thing…I'm going to stop by to visit Keira in about an hour. I won't remember this conversation, so please don't mention it."

"Why won't you…" Colby stopped midsentence when Ann raised her arm in front of him. A scar stretched from the middle of her palm to her elbow. That's when he noticed the other signs: slightly longer hair, clothing more conservative than usual, and a modest engagement ring on her left hand.

"You're not the Ann from my time, are you?"

She turned toward the back door, but stopped in the middle of the yard. "And, Colby, just a word of advice…don't underestimate Nana. She's no grandmother and is as sly as they come."

She continued through the kitchen, proud of the way she had handled the situation. She felt strong and respected. It was exactly the way that her mother told her it would be on that night several years ago. She remembered it like it just happened yesterday. She thought she had gone insane as she watched her first birthday from the corner of the living room. It was her Dad's way of breaking the news about her family's extraordinary abilities. Something a little more conservative may have been easier to digest.

Later she would learn that it was tradition to keep their true nature secret until the eldest of the next generation reached their fifteenth birthday. Keira had been brought up to know that she was something more than human; Ann had it thrust upon her. As Ann looked upon her injured friend, she pondered which was better. Hopefully what she had done today was enough to nudge things in the right direction without consequences. She took a deep breath as she faded back to the future with a sonic boom.

***

After just ten days of recuperation, Keira was back to one hundred percent. She awoke as the sun peered through the blinds of her bedroom window. She spotted Colby sleeping on a bean bag chair in the corner. His mouth gaped open wide as he snored. She pulled a quilt over him, grabbed a change of clothes, and slipped out of the bedroom to take a shower and brush her teeth. She had already returned and was seated on the end of the bed when he stirred.

"I think you can clock out now, Dr. Hayes," Keira smirked. "I'm all better."

"You look great."

He just blurted it out without thinking. His cheeks turned red as his waking mind caught up with his mouth.

"Really? Well, what can I say? It takes more than the supreme ruler of an ancient, evil empire to get me down," she joked. She sounded like her old self.

Colby joined her on the edge of the bed. His face was serious. "I guess you don't need me anymore. I better get home."

She put a hand on his shoulder. "I'll always need you," she whispered. "Thank you." She brushed her fingers on his cheek.

"You're welcome."

He jumped up and headed toward the exit. Just as Colby reached the bedroom door, he turned. Keira noticed his stop in her peripheral vision and looked up. He met her gaze and stood silent for a moment.

"You remember the conversation we had…the one on the day you met your parents?" he asked.

"Maybe."

She did. It was completely embarrassing. She had been scared and crazy with jealousy. She had told him that she loved him. She told him that she wanted him and he said nothing. She would never forget that day.

He stared her down until she came forward with the truth. "Okay, okay, I remember, but I wish I could forget," she finally admitted.

"Well, I haven't forgotten," he said with a smirk. He walked out of the room and headed for the front door.

Keira stepped after him. She reached to stop him and, forgetting her own strength, spun him completely around.

"Whoa," he countered. His arms were spread out to re-balance himself.

Keira wrapped her fingers around his upper arms and looked into his eyes. It was then that she realized she had no idea what to say.

He stood for a moment gazing back into her chocolate brown eyes. Then he laughed, "I can't believe it…you're….you're speechless."

She dropped her hands and crossed them at her chest with a step back. "I am not speechless."

"Keira."

She took a half step forward, "Colby."

He took a half step forward, "Keira."

She put her hands on her hips in frustration, but he kept his gaze on her. He inched closer. His breath was steady. He leaned to her slowly. She closed her eyes.

He brushed past her lips to her ear. Breathlessly, he whispered, "When I'm not with you, I feel broken and all I can think about is the next time that I'll see you."

"Sounds familiar," she said opening one eye.

"Yeah, I heard that line before. It's a little cheesy, but I'm thinking that cheese is probably a good way to sweep a tooth mouse off her feet." He kissed her on the forehead and made his way to the front door.

Shock. That's the best way to describe it. She was in complete shock. She hadn't seen this coming. She didn't move a muscle or utter a word as he said goodbye to Nana and left. She didn't know how she really felt about Colby now, after everything, but she would need to decide…soon.

Once Colby closed the door behind him, Nana ushered Keira back to her bedroom for some rest before dinner. She was healed, but didn't want to overdo it; so, she didn't put up a fight. She entered her room and closed the door, pausing with her hand on the knob for a moment to take a deep breath.

"I wish you no harm." Someone rustled behind her.

She spun around into a defensive posture. The sun was setting, streaming its last golden orange light into her darkened bedroom. There, standing by the head of her bed, was William. His hands were raised in the air, fingers spread, to show that he had no weapons. His hair was ruffled, clothes disheveled, and he looked as though he hadn't shaved in days.

"Talk fast," she ordered. She reached for her dagger before realizing that she hadn't strapped it back on after her shower.

"Keira, please, it's me."

"I don't know you, mogdoc." She eased along the wall to her dresser. The dagger, still in its sheath, lay in her view.

He had seen the weapon and made no move to prevent her from retrieving it. He intentionally ignored her advance as he said to the floor, "This is what I know. You were one of four kids that the Emperor thought could be the guardian from the prophecy. He ordered me to get close to you so that he could discover the truth."

"And then your giant ego botched things up." She picked up the dagger and pointed it toward him.

"Is that what you think? I knew that I had to break it off. I knew it was you. You were always so protective of him and then that day, the day the police took him, you pushed me." He couldn't look at her. He closed his eyes, summoning the memory of that day. "You were so strong, that's when it all clicked."

Keira pretended not to care about what he was saying. She stood frozen against the wall. "If you really knew, then why didn't your Daddy just come and get me? Why did you dump me?"

He pleaded, "Listen to what I'm saying. How can you not understand? Can't you see? I love you. I told them that it wasn't you. I stayed away to protect you."

Keira huffed. Why did everyone think they had to abandon her to protect her? Then it all became very clear. He must know what her parents did. He would know how to use that information to further his own agenda. Now, Keira was not angry, she was mad. He was a mogdoc. Mogdocs don't love. They plot. They manipulate. They lie.

"I can't believe that you controlled my emotions like that. You made me believe that I…" Her eyes narrowed on him. "Get out of my house." With that, the last bit of sun disappeared under the horizon.

"No, that's the other thing. I couldn't calm you down. I thought you liked me because I was willing it, but when the police took Colby, I couldn't calm you. I know because I tried. I really, really tried and it didn't work. My power doesn't work on guardians." In the darkness, he rushed to her with inhuman speed. Standing before her, he whispered, "Think about it, if I could control your emotions, we would be holding each other and I would be kissing you softly right now."

Keira trembled with anger and fear. "Get...out...now..."

"Please, I didn't know about their plan to capture you and Colby. I rushed to you as soon as I found out."

"Now!"

"I saved your life," he reasoned. "I disobeyed my father. I fought my big sister. That has to mean something to you."

She pushed him back with the dagger. "Your big sis? She's my age. Are you lying about the little things now too?"

"She was already masquerading as a human. I guess she thought, why not be a younger human. Yes, she really is that vain."

He pulled back to sit again on the edge of the bed. He laughed despite himself and took that same old shy look to the ground. It used to make her smile when he did that, now it just hurt. He was trying to be lovable; still she knew he couldn't be trusted. Though he was right about one thing; he saved her life. Broo would have killed her if he hadn't stepped in.

She lowered her dagger a few inches. "Listen, I haven't told the others about you. Consider that repayment for saving my life. We are even. I never want to see you again."

"So, you're protecting me?"

"No, I'm repaying a life debt. Consider it paid in full."

"Keira, I know I've had to lie to you. But what we had was real. You and I are one and the same. I've loved you since our first date. You know that. Please remember."

She remembered loving him. It was painful to remember. She felt her spirit die a little on the day of that ill-fated Christmas shopping trip. A little more died the day she heard Brooke call him brother. But, a thought kept trotting through her head. Could she trust her feelings? She was half human. Maybe he had at least some power over her. She pushed everything down so that it burned in her stomach. He would not control her now. She wouldn't let him. Her voice was sharp and cold. Her words, so cruel, that they left a bad taste in her mouth. "Go back to your cave, mogdoc."

"I can't, not without your help."

"Right and why would I help you, William, or whatever your name is?"

"My name is Brun Gammen, true Emperor of the Mogdoc Empire, and I need you to fulfill your destiny."

"No, these are just more lies. Gammen named Brooke as his successor. I heard it myself."

"He was wrong. He knew that the title passes to the eldest male, not to his precious little princess. She was always his favorite."

"No." Keira couldn't believe what she was hearing. She didn't want to hear it.

"Keira, please, Broo's trying to contest my crown. The Sect was present during father's declaration, so they have sworn their allegiance to her. While they aren't blood royals, their influence carries much weight. Keira, I can't let her take over. I've spent too much time living as a human. I can't go back to the way things have always been. I have a responsibility to teach my people that there is a better way."

Even though his words were persuasive, Keira hung tight to a single truth. Mogdocs are master manipulators. He had another agenda and she could see it peeking through his words.

"So you want me to get her out of the way for you? What's wrong? Don't want to get your hands dirty, your highness? I won't be your hired gun."

"I'm not asking you to kill my sister. I'm asking you to use the human gift. Take me down too. I don't need to be ruler; I just need the crown out of her reach. When she and the Sect are gone, then I can bring peace between humans and mogdocs and we can be together."

"Together? You're insane. That's not going to happen."

"You and I are meant to be together. I know this. I know it with all my soul."

"Just stop it! Stop it! You don't have a soul."

"I do, but it's lost without you."

"Oh, please. Was that supposed to sound romantic?"

"It's the truth."

Keira, tired of the lies and grand romantic pretenses, had finally reached her limit. She raised her dagger.

"There is no truth in this room right now. Look at you. You come to me, hiding in the shadows, disguised as human, whispering lies with a forked tongue, telling me what you think I want to hear. You may look like someone I once loved, but you are a savage, revolting mogdoc. I will NEVER forget that. The William that I knew…"

He swept behind her in the blink of an eye. Wrapping his arms around her tightly, he whispered in her ear, "The William you love…"

That was the wrong thing to say. She pulled the dagger above her shoulder to his throat. "Just try me, mogdoc. You think I loved you? I loved William, but it doesn't matter. He never really existed."

She took a deep breath and straightened her shoulders. "Get out and don't come back," she growled, yet her bottom lip was quivering.

"Make no mistake; I will not let you forget. You are mine."

He sniffed her hair. It smelled of honeysuckle shampoo and reminded him of the gazebo from their first date. He clenched his jaw as he let go and lifted his left hand to slice a tear in reality. He stepped into it and disappeared.

Keira collapsed on the bed. She couldn't think. She couldn't breathe. Were his last words a plea or a threat? Was he lying? Did it matter? Regardless, he still risked his family and position to save her life. He probably jeopardized everything just to come to her tonight. Beyond it all, she knew he was right. Despite everything, she still loved him.

Chapter 24: The Birthday Party

Keira worked her way through her crowded backyard with a platter full of raw hamburgers. For every person she knew, there were at least three that she didn't know. Yet, they all seemed to know her and call her by name. A white-haired man stopped her at the back door to congratulate her on completing her first year of high school. A skinny blond stopped her at the garden gate to ask where she could find Nana. Finally, Keira could see her goal. August was standing at the barbeque, clad in a "Licensed to Grill" apron, waiting for her arrival. He was excited to take on this fatherly tradition, a perfectly normal human duty.

Keira rushed toward him, hoping to not be stopped again. Two excited boys, playing tag, ran past her and she lifted the platter above her head to avoid an incident. The younger, an especially mischievous sun kissed-blond, grabbed onto her waist and tried to use her as a human shield. As the other boy came close, he pushed her, which threw her out of balance and launched the tray full of burgers into the air. She twirled around and caught herself, the tray, and the food. When she came to a stop her nose was just inches away from Colby's face.

"Smooth."

Keira straightened and handed the platter to her father.

"Thank you, sweetheart," August said.

"Where'd you come from?" Keira asked Colby.

"Oh, I've been here for a while, just catching up with your Dad."

"See you later, Colby," August nodded, giving them a convenient exit.

Colby took Keira's hand. The half moon hung high in a cloudless sky. The backyard was magic and full of life. White lights twinkled in the shrubs and trees. Little magical beings that looked like pinpoints of blue light (Nana called them will 'o wisps) danced and chased each other above the crowd. A few guests brought guitars and assorted alien-looking instruments. They started an impromptu jam session on the back porch. Their music filled the air. Colby was dazzled by all that surrounded him. He hadn't even noticed that Keira had led him back to the house. They walked inside and sat at the kitchen table, overlooking the backyard crowd.

"I can't believe there are so many people here," Colby commented. "Oh wait, that sounded bad. I didn't mean that Nana doesn't have any friends."

"Don't worry. I was thinking the same thing. I think that most of them are of the magical variety. I don't know any of these people."

"Really? They know you. I heard several of them talking. They're very complimentary. If they don't even know you, you must be developing a stellar reputation."

"Me?"

"Yes, I suppose you are becoming sort of a warrior princess of the tooth fairies," he laughed.

"Shut up, someone is going to hear you. Anyway, they should be here for Nana. It's her birthday after all."

"Speaking of Nana, how old is she?"

She had been waiting for him to ask. "Five hundred and she just earned her fifth tail, so it's a big deal."

She meant for her response to jar Colby. She enjoyed seeing him squirm. Behind his composure, she could almost see the debate raging in his head…should he shrug it off or should he ask? Finally, his curiosity gave in.

"Tail, huh?"

"Yeah, it's not her ninth, but five are still very powerful." She wasn't going to help him out on this one.

However, Colby was not so quick to give up. "So she's a…"

Keira didn't respond. She just sat smiling.

Colby could see that trying to solicit the answer from her was useless. He mulled it over. "She's a tooth fairy too?"

"Try again."

In his head, he rummaged through stories of fictional characters…ones with tails. "Is she a werewolf?"

You're getting warmer."

"Ok, maybe not a werewolf, but a were-something?"

Keira was enjoying this a little too much. She knew that the perfectly normal Colby would never identify the perfectly abnormal and rare creature that she called Nana. So, out of guilt, she decided to help. "You're pretty much right. She turns into a fox." She quickly corrected herself, "Sort of a magical fox."

"Magical fox," Colby repeated thoughtfully.

"She's actually a kitsune. She can turn from fox to human as she likes and she has some other awesome powers."

"Okay, now you're just pulling my leg."

"No, it's true. In her fox form, she has five tails and with each new tail, she gets a new power. Nine's the most I've ever heard of."

"So she just got a new power?" Colby asked, allowing himself to believe Keira's explanation.

"Possession. I'm hoping it's not as creepy as it sounds."

"Sure."

"That was a little too fast, wasn't it? Too much information?"

"No. It's just really different. I guess it doesn't come as a complete shock that a prodigal guardian would have a magical caretaker," he validated, trying to shake off his uneasiness. "She's five hundred, huh?"

"Yeah, cool huh?" Keira said, but she noticed Colby's expression change. "Why the face?"

"Sorry. That's great for her, but…"

"But?"

"I was just wondering if you will leave me behind when I'm tottering along with a walker and you're still young and beautiful."

Keira couldn't help but blush at the word 'beautiful'. Even with all her confidence, she had never thought of herself that way.

She took his hand across the table and stroked it a couple of times. Then she turned it over, palm up. She traced the lines of his palm slowly with her finger as she spoke. "Remember when we were three and we got into your mom's makeup?"

He nodded.

She continued, "Remember when we were five and I dragged you into the classroom on our first day of kindergarten?"

He nodded again.

"Remember when we were eight and we had our first camping trip in the backyard?"

He nodded again, this time with a chuckle.

"I'm not a kitsune. I age the same as you, the same as any human," she smiled and looked up into his eyes. She took one hand away and reached in her pocket before continuing, "But guardians have access to a place where time moves slower. A guardian can even take a human there, although it's sort of frowned upon. Anyway, guardians aren't immortal, but spending some time across the barrier has an advantage."

She held up a leather cord bracelet with a dime-sized, stamped copper piece dangling from it. The pseudo coin had strange markings and the universal symbol for eternity etched upon it.

"Hey, that looks like the good luck charm that your Mom gave me before the showdown with Bov." He examined it, "But this one's a little different."

"It's called an Atlantis token."

"Oh, so it's *magically* lucky?"

She laughed. It felt good to laugh, but she felt it most prudent to continue. "Well, you've heard of Atlantis, right?"

"Sure, the lost city of Atlantis. The city was, I think, swallowed up by the sea, or something like that."

"The version that I was told goes a little differently, but it starts the same as any other bedtime story…"

Once upon a time…

A band of explorers were returning home after a long journey. Their expedition had taken more than two decades to complete. They now were making their way through Greece. Once they reached Athens, it would only be a few days more by ship to reach their homeland. When they, at last, reached the city, the weary travelers sought supplies and a night's refuge before embarking on the final leg of their journey.

They found the city of Athens to be glorious and progressive. The citizens welcomed the strangers with open arms, even though they were creatures, like none they had ever seen before. Mogdoc was the name they grunted. The guttural name bubbled up from the primordial mud out of which they crawled. Of course, that's not how they made their first impression.

They looked like monsters, but they were not judged on appearance. The kind-hearted people embraced their differences and took them in. They gave them warm food, cold drink, and soft beds. The mogdocs, no longer thinking of home, found excuses to stay first one night, then another, and another.

On the third night, the mogdocs were the special guests of a general in the Athenian army. The youngest female mogdoc, equivalent to a human of 6-years-old, had become fast friends with the general's daughter. They spent every waking moment together. They skipped arm-in-arm, shared toys, and even played tea party with sweet drink and cake. On that night, the third night, the young mogdoc snuck out of bed for a midnight snack. She crept down the stairs, stole an apple from the kitchen, and slipped into the rose garden. To her astonishment, her friend, the general's daughter was already there. The young girl was seated on a concrete bench at the garden's edge. As the mogdoc got closer, she could see that the girl was crying. A rose thorn had pierced her finger. The tiny mogdoc took her finger, pulled out the thorn, and sniffed the blood.

In those days, mogdocs carried pouches of healing herbs. The elder mogdocs still carry them today as a reminder of this story. This young mogdoc had one and immediately delved into it. She pulled out some sweet smelling herbs and wrapped them around her friend's finger. This made the young girl feel better. She hugged her mogdoc friend before returning to bed.

The next morning, the girl told her father of how the curious stranger had nursed her finger. The general was delighted and in gratitude invited the mogdoc clan to extend their stay. So, over the next few days, the mogdocs continued to stay at the general's home. The children's midnight meeting in the garden became a nightly occurrence. On the sixth night, the mogdoc was the first to arrive in the garden. The human girl skipped to the bench. The young mogdoc smiled at her friend and offered her a bite of her midnight snack. The general's daughter screamed in horror. There was no apple. That night's midnight snack was a human infant, blue and drained of blood. The young mogdoc took delight in the girl's fear. She slashed the girl's neck and fed from her friend until she was no more.

This story has been handed down from generation to generation as a testament to the manipulative nature of the mogdocs and the evil found in even the youngest of their kind. The mogdoc child had befriended the human girl to gain access. She had played tea party to sweeten the blood. She had healed her a few nights before out of greed, in order to save every drop of blood until the time was right.

The next morning, there was no way to cover up the sins of the young mogdoc. The creatures were expelled from the city and fled into the sea. However, the mogdocs were not humbled by their punishment. When they reached their home port, their story only fanned a flame of contempt. Mogdoc hatred for humans and lust for human blood soon grew out of control. A great naval power, the mogdoc city of Atlantis amassed their fleet on a mission to destroy humankind, starting with the city of Athens.

Thankfully, the Athenians won the battle and successfully defended their home, but at great cost. The beautiful city was left in ruin. Many died that day and it was certain that the beasts would try again. The few survivors gathered at a fountain near the heart of the city. That is when the surviving guardians made the drastic decision to stop the spread of the mogdoc *scourge and protect the human race at all cost. It was a decision that would change the world forever. They cast a spell. It was magic so epic that it had never been performed successfully before or since. With the spell, they banished Atlantis and the entire continent upon which it stood; effectively sealing off humans from the Mogdoc Empire. Only the guardians could walk on both sides of the barrier that separated the two.*

Keira held the coin up to the light.

As the last word of the spell was spoken, the city of Atlantis shook and the waters of the Atlantic swirled above the highest tower. Fear rocked the citizens for an entire day and into the night. By midnight, it was over and Atlantis was gone. Knowing that the empire was forever banished from the Earth into its own realm, the Athenians took a cleansing breath of relief. But it didn't last.

The strongest magic is based in passion, so the survivors cast their spell in haste while emotions were still running high. They did not immediately foresee the consequences of their actions.

As they began to assess the damage done during the great battle; they quickly realized that there was more missing than dead. The mogdocs had taken prisoners. These humans were now trapped by the magic intended to save them. The survivors were lucky that the banishment spell worked the first time. There was no guarantee that they could do it again. Knowing that it would be too dangerous to re-introduce the Mogdoc Empire back into the world, the survivors cast a second spell. This time they used the only thing that had not been destroyed by the attack. It was the only thing they had in abundant supply, the coins from the

fountain at the city's center. They charmed the coins;
allowing any human who holds one to pass through
the barrier between this world and Atlantis. Then the
guardians, who could pass between the realms, seeded
the coins in the mogdoc dungeons. They weren't able
to free everyone, but many were saved by their efforts.

Keira held the coin still. Colby couldn't help
but notice that it didn't shimmer or sparkle or really do
anything significant. From afar it just looked like an
old, smashed penny.

"On the continent of Atlantis, time moves
slower. It's a side effect from the spell. Some
guardians even have homes in the mountains above the
city; allowing them to avoid mogdocs, but still get the
anti-aging benefits. Mom and Dad live in a village
near one of the peaks. From what I understand,
humans, especially charges, are not usually allowed
because of the danger, but it seems that Dad is really
good at getting what he wants."

"I can't argue that."

"Yeah, well, even though you didn't know
what it was at the time, Mom let you borrow her token
so that you could cross the barrier to meet Bov."

"But we went to Dubai, not to some banished
magical city."

She nodded, waiting for him to catch up.

"Oh, I get it. When we started out, we didn't
know where we would end up."

"Yeah, we didn't know where the threshold
was going to lead. If you tried to go through the
mogdoc's threshold and it led to Atlantis, you
wouldn't have been able to pass through the barrier.
You would have been stuck in between."

Colby very visibly gulped. "Wait a sec, if nothing but guardians and coin-holding humans can get through, then why do we have a mogdoc problem?"

"Bo Gammen, Bov's father, found a way around the spell so that Bov could pass through. There are those that have kept an eye on him, but it was only him that could cross the barrier. One mogdoc wasn't enough to cause worry, but it looks like he has improved upon his father's design. He pulled the whole Sect of Low through the barrier like it was nothing. If they figure out how to transport an army or even destroy the barrier entirely…"

"It won't come to that. Wait," he stared away thinking, focusing on the picture in his memory.

"What?"

Colby shook his head. "He didn't pull the Sect through. He just pulled me and I was wearing your mom's token. *She* brought the Sect through the barrier. They were holding on to her as they passed through."

Keira hadn't realized it before, but he was right. Yet, in her mind, it didn't change anything. "Now is the time to put an end to it."

Colby lowered his head. He knew immediately where this conversation was leading. "Go ahead, I know there's more to it," he mumbled.

"They know who I am now and they've attacked. My parents are going home so that they can rally support in case we need it. They plan to leave in three days. "

"And you're going to miss them?" Colby suggested hopefully.

"Having the warrior princess of the tooth fairies pleading her case in person is bound to solicit better results, don't you think?"

"You're going with them?"

She ignored the question and concentrated on the coin. "Like I said before, these coins are very rare. Two nights ago, Dad gave me this one. It belonged to my great grandfather," she said dangling the flattened coin. "This is the only one I'll ever own. And now it belongs to you."

"I...uh...," Colby stumbled.

"Speechless?"

"Keira, I can't..."

She looked deep into his blue eyes. "I want you to have it," she said slipping it into his palm. He held it tightly and nodded.

"Whew," she jumped up from her chair. "Too much drama, bring on the birthday cake!"

SNEAK PEEK

Keep reading for a special sneak preview of Book 2 in the Midnight Guardian Series coming Summer 2011.

Someone had left the window open. The warm, summer air wafted through the darkened bedroom. An overstuffed teddy bear was the only witness as the light grew brighter and brighter.

"And then you lift the child like so," he placed a hand under the child's back and elevated her slightly.

"Or like this." Keira took hold of the sleeping girl's wrists and waved them side to side, mimicking hula dancing.

Arden glared at her. She rolled her eyes, but lowered the girl's arms. Keira stood up and moved away as he continued.

"Then in one hand, you hold the vox and position it directly in front of the sternum. Hold it against the charge's body." A thick British accent lent his speech a condescending edge.

"Yeah, I got it," Keira whispered as she wandered absentmindedly to the window.

He looked to her. "Are you even paying attention?"

"Kid. Vox. Coil. I said I got it," she huffed without a look at him.

"The vox takes several minutes to pass. However, after it completely dissipates, do not dilly-dally. Release the child for the coil will manifest itself promptly."

"Duh."

Arden jerked his head up. "What the...

Keira thought he was responding to her comment until she turned to see the glowing green eyes and a burst of crimson. A mogdoc, hidden within the canopy above the bed, had lowered itself and surprised Arden. It slashed his cheek, causing him to drop the vox. Arden smacked the creature into the wall with so much force that its head broke through the drywall. The commotion woke the child. Startled, she screamed and knocked the vox from the blankets onto the floor. The mogdoc seized her and scrambled up the bed post. It dangled her by the neck from its perch on the canopy crossbeams. The girl kicked the air, gasping for breath. So strong, the creature held her neck in a single hand as it clung to the canopy with the other.

Keira could hear worried shouts as rushed footsteps hit the hallway. She leapt to the door and locked it. "Hurry, Arden. The parents are coming!" She braced the door as the girl's parents started to beat against it. Their frantic voices were muffled; Keira turned her attention back to the bed.

Arden, with a dagger in hand, stood on the mattress. His dark brown eyes were locked on the mogdoc, waiting for an opening. Seeing that he had the upper hand, the mogdoc wickedly smiled. It pressed its thumb into the girl's neck. The sharp thumbnail pierced her skin. The girl's eyes widened as the creature lowered its head to lick the drops of blood that escaped. Keira felt as though the world fell into slow motion, but only seconds passed. The mogdoc tightened its grip and a tear ran down the girl's cheek. She stopped struggling and gasped one last time. Satisfied, it dropped her limp body. The creature shrieked triumphantly and dove out the open window into the night.

Fury flamed in Keira's eyes. She pulled a dagger from her boot and rushed after the creature.

"Wait," Arden ordered.

The door was quiet. *The parents probably went to get help or find an ax or something*, Keira thought. She didn't want to be there when they came back and saw that their daughter was…no, she couldn't even think it.

"It's getting away," Keira pleaded, but instead of following, she stopped, fixed by the sight of the child in Arden's arms. She looked like a doll with eyes closed and mouth open.

"There's a pulse and she's breathing again. There's still time," he said. "Get the vox."

"It doesn't heal," Keira said as she reached under the bed and lifted it to him.

"I know."

He placed the vox to the girl's chest. Its light slowly disappeared and the wind picked up. He lowered the girl to the bed.

"What are you doing? We have to take her with us."

"That is not permitted."

"She needs help. She'll die."

"I said no." He grabbed Keira's hand. She kicked him, but he was stronger. Arden yanked her into the coil and they were gone.

ABOUT THE AUTHOR

After graduating with the honor of Outstanding Communications Student from the University of Rio Grande in southeastern Ohio, Bryna Butler settled down with her high school sweetheart on their family farm along the banks of the Ohio River. Life on the farm is never dull, especially with their two young sons who fearlessly provide constant entertainment.